Swimming Upstream

John Watson

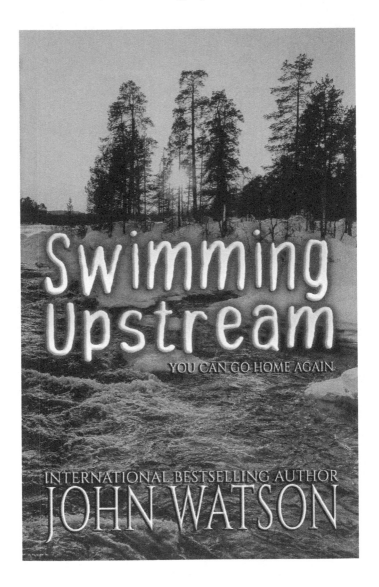

Dedication

This is a love story to the place I will always call home and to the friends who will forever have my back. I'm looking at you, Gary Sweeney.

I would stand there by the filling tide
till Preshal bowed his stallion head.
And if the two of us were together
on the shores of Calgary in Mull
between Scotland and Tiree,
between this world and eternity,
I'd stand there till time was done
counting the sands grain by grain.
—Sorley McLean

Chapter One

The lines and notations on the blueprints scattered across his desk began to meld together to create a kaleidoscopic pattern of which he could make no sense. Tossing his glasses on top of the papers, Greig Ramsay pinched the bridge of his nose and turned away from his desk, looking out across the Atlanta skyline through his floor-to-ceiling office windows.

Thick, black clouds that looked like charcoal-colored cotton candy drifted lazily across the skyscrapers, threatening a deluge of rain. The clouds reminded Greig of Scotland, the home he had left a decade ago to pursue a career as an architect. He had been the top student in his class, and when offered a position in the States, he jumped at the opportunity for adventure, not particularly caring that he had left a family and a girlfriend in his wake.

When he first arrived at Charles Harrison Studios, there had been talk of nepotism given that the owner was also originally from Scotland. Those rumors quickly ceased as Greig proved his worth, bringing in new clients at a steady clip and swiftly climbing the corporate ladder. The corner office in which he now sat was one that he had more than earned. He also knew that the company would be his when old man Harrison retired, which was coming sooner rather than later.

Turning back to his desk, Greig picked up his Blackberry and checked for messages for the thousandth time that morning. His wife, Lisa, was pregnant and ready to go into labor at any minute. Harrison had tried to talk Greig into taking a couple of weeks off, but he knew that staying at home and fussing over his wife would only make her crazy.

Rolling up the blueprints, he set them aside and flipped open his laptop to scan his email inbox, which seemed to fill up any time he looked away for even a fleeting moment. As he began to respond to the important messages, a knock at his office door pulled him away from the task.

"Come in."

The door flew open, and Charles Harrison came striding in, a broad smile plastered across his gaunt, heavily lined face. "Any word on the wee one?" he asked, plopping himself in a leather chair in the corner of the office.

"Nothing yet," Greig sighed. "I swear this kid is not interested in making an appearance any time soon."

The old man laughed as he reached into his vest and pulled out a pocket watch. "The weatherman says we are in for a big storm this afternoon. Why don't you call it a day and go home before it hits? I don't like the idea of you driving on I-85 in the middle of all that."

Greig smiled and thought about how his relationship with Charles was more of a father/son situation than the one he had with his real dad. The two men couldn't be any more different if they tried;

where Charles oozed sophistication and always looked dapper in a three-piece suit, John Ramsay was a cardigan and slippers man who always had a dirty joke at the ready. He loved them both in different ways, but he felt closer to his boss. "I really need to finish up the approval of the Banner account before I head out," Greig said, sneaking another glance at his Blackberry.

"Nonsense. Get one of your staff to do it. When you take over the company, I want you to spend as much time away from this office as possible. I don't need to be here at all, but I can't stay away. It's why I'm single and have no wee ones of my own. I don't want you falling into that bad work habit, Greig."

The thought of working from home was one that appealed to Greig, but like his boss, he felt drawn to the office. There was something about the buzz of activity and seeing new projects come to fruition that excited him. The month off after his child's birth would probably prove to be a deciding factor in how he moved forward. "I'd love to spend as much time as possible with Lisa and my boy."

"Then do it. You've worked so hard to get to where you are, so hire well and delegate as needed," Charles said, rising from the chair with a groan. "Any ideas on a name yet?"

"We're thinking of Graham."

"That's a fine name, and you'll make a fine father, my boy." Charles moved to the office door but stopped for a moment and turned to face Greig. "Now get your arse home as quickly as possible. That's a long bloody drive."

As soon as Charles left the office, Greig turned back to the window and stared at the clouds as the first few drops of rain began to patter against the glass. He had made a habit of not looking down, the dizzying height of his office not something that made him feel particularly comfortable. Decision made, he pulled on his jacket, tucked the blueprints under his arm, and headed out, closing his office door on the way.

Stopping by the desk of his assistant, Greig told her to forward all messages to his cell. Head down, he bolted for the elevators, hoping he could move quickly enough as not to get pulled into a conversation. He popped his head into Charles' office, which sat right by the elevators and let him know he was leaving.

By the time he pulled out of the underground parking lot, fat drops of rain were coming down hard. The downtown streets were mostly free of traffic, which was a blessing, but by the time he reached I-285, traffic was beginning to pile up. Foot on the gas, Greig weaved in and out of traffic, trying to outrun the storm that was on his tail and closing fast.

He had to hit the brakes hard when he hit the bridge that connected to I-85. While the highway below looked clear, traffic had come to a halt on the ramp. Flashing lights at the entrance told the story, as three lanes tried to merge into one as vehicles maneuvered around the crash at the bottom.

Greig edged his car forward, letting out a groan as the skies opened up and the vehicles on the highway slowed down, flashers blinking as drivers tried to navigate the slick surface. It was barely gone noon, but the dark skies gave the appearance of night.

BOOM!

"Jesus suffering fuck," Greig yelled as a massive thunderclap tore through the sky, rocking the car. Lightning flashed, followed by another peal of thunder that somehow seemed louder than the first.

The rain fell harder, the drops hammering against the car and drowning out the sound of the radio, which was playing some light jazz. Greig powered off the stereo and inched a little closer to the highway as two more cars made their way around the collision at the bottom of the on-ramp.

He jumped again as his phone in the driver's seat began to ring. Snatching the Blackberry up, his breath hitched when he saw Lisa's name displayed on the screen. "Is everything okay?" he yelled into the phone, panting hard.

"I'm fine, babe. You don't sound so good. Is that secretary of yours chasing you around the office again?"

"What? No, I'm stuck in bloody traffic."

"Let me guess, Charles pushed you out the door," Lisa giggled.

"He did. I wasn't getting much done. Besides, I'd sooner be home with you. How are you feeling?"

"Tired. That boy of yours is playing soccer again. Either that or he wants out pretty badly."

Greig peered through the rain and saw a tow truck moving a mangled vehicle off the ramp and onto the highway, speeding off and allowing traffic to start moving again. "Well, tell him to stay where he is until I get home. I'm just about to hit 85 now, so I should only be another twenty or thirty minutes."

"You be careful on that road; it sounds nasty out there. I love you."

"I love you, too. Go get some rest."

Closing the call, Greig flipped the phone onto the passenger seat and eased onto the highway, resisting the urge to gun it and get home. Thoughts of his wife and unborn son flooded his mind, bringing a smile to his face, but he pushed them aside as he focused on the road ahead. He'd see them both soon enough.

Chapter Two

By the time Greig pushed the garage door opener button, the rain was down to a misty drizzle that looked like spiderwebs falling from the sky. He eased the car into the garage, pulled out his work stuff, and bounded up the three small stairs leading into the house.

Dropping his stuff on the kitchen island, he walked through to the den, where he found his wife asleep on the couch, her mouth hanging open and a trail of drool sliding down her cheek. Smiling, he knelt beside her and brushed her blonde bangs to the side, feeling the sweat on her brow as he did so. Even with the air conditioning blasting out cool air, Lisa still gave off heat like a furnace. Greig had made the mistake of complaining about the house temperature once, after which she blasted him with a tirade about carrying his child and destroying her body so that he could have a boy. He knew better than to mention it after that, choosing the wiser option of layering as though he was going on a fall hike.

Lisa stirred under his touch and opened her eyes, her icy blue irises matching the room temperature. "You made it home safe. Yay."

"How could you ever doubt my superior driving skills? I'll tell you what, though, you wouldn't have liked that drive."

Lisa reached out and grabbed his hand, squeezing it. "Oh, come on, you know I love riding with you. That's how I ended up in this delicate condition, my delicious highlander man."

"You need to stop reading those bloody romance novels. What I was going to tell you, before you got all dirty on me, was that I got stuck up on the bridge on 285."

Sitting up on the sofa, Lisa let out a little giggle. "I love when you say dirty. It's so damn cute, but that bridge, nuh-uh. I would have freaked out."

"Maybe the scare would have frightened the wee man out of his hidey-hole," Greig said, placing a hand on his wife's belly.

"Well, I've heard that sex at this stage in the pregnancy can speed things along. Care to put it to the test?"

"Your wish is my command, m'lady."

"Okay, lover boy, but I'm going to need a pizza after the fact. I've been craving one all day."

Greig smiled and helped Lisa to her feet. "Plundering and pepperoni it is. Now, let's get you upstairs to the bedroom."

***

Slipping on a pair of sweatpants and an old soccer jersey, Greig snuck out of the room while Lisa dozed. He called the local pizza joint and placed a pick-up order, shuddering involuntarily when requesting pineapple on one half of the pie. Greig was of the belief that pineapple had no place on a pizza, something that Lisa also believed until her second trimester. Now it was all pineapple, all the time. He hoped it was a craving that would vanish the moment their child made it into the world.

He plucked the car keys off the island and headed out to the car, hoping the sound of the garage door opening wouldn't rouse Lisa from her slumber. He toyed with the idea of leaving it open, but while Lawrenceton was a quiet little town and their neighborhood a good one, he still couldn't bring himself to do it. Closing the garage door, he pulled out of the driveway and headed for the downtown area's pizza shop.

It wasn't until he was sitting in the shop's waiting area that he realized he had forgotten to pick up his Blackberry. Cursing quietly, he stepped up to the counter and rang the service bell, the sound bringing an acne-scarred teenager out of the kitchen area.

"What's up, dude? You here for a pick-up?"

"I just spoke to you five minutes ago. Is my pizza almost ready? It's for Ramsay."

"Boxing it up now, chief. Do you want to pay?"

Greig's hand trembled as he reached into his wallet and pulled out a couple of twenties, way more than was necessary. "Keep the change, but please get me the pizza. I need to get home to my wife."

The kid smirked. "Ah, the old ball and chain cracking the whip."

Resisting the urge to smack the teenager upside the head, Greig grinned and said, "Something like that. Can I please get the pizza now?"

"That's some accent, dude. You an Aussie?" the kid asked as he shuffled back to the kitchen area, his sneakers scuffing the floor with each slow step.

Blood boiling, Greig balled his fists and shoved them into the pockets of his sweatpants. "I'm Scottish," he said through gritted teeth.

The kid plopped the pizza box on the counter. "Super cool, my third uncle is Scottish."

"Cool, so is mine," Greig snapped as he snatched up the box and bolted out the door.

The five-minute drive home felt like an eternity, with every traffic light set to red for much longer than usual. As he pulled into the driveway, Greig yelled at the garage door to hurry up as it trundled along the track like a sloth pulling itself along a tree branch.

Grabbing the pizza, he ran inside the house, just in time to hear the text tone playing on his phone. Lisa stood just beyond the kitchen, bent over double, her grey pajama bottoms soaked at the crotch. She tossed her phone onto the couch and grabbed her belly with both hands.

"Are you alright, baby?" Greig asked, instantly realizing it was a stupid question.

"My water broke," Lisa hissed. "Seems that whole sex thing might be right after all."

Bounding across the hardwood and almost slipping on the puddle spreading out from her feet, Greig took his wife gently by the elbow and started leading her to the garage. "Let's get you in the car, and then I'll grab your bag. Everything you need is in there, right?"

"Yes, but you need to call my doctor, too. I need her at the hospital."

"No worries, I'll call once we are on the road."

Helping his wife into the passenger seat, Greig hopped in on the other side and started the car, turning the air conditioning on full blast. He then ran back into the house, snatched up the overnight bag from the closet beside the garage door, and made it back in a matter of seconds, his heart hammering in his chest. "Are you ready, love?"

"As ready as I'm ever going to be."

Nodding grimly, Greig tore out of the garage and turned the vehicle in the direction of the hospital, hitting the speed dial on the Blackberry as he went.

Chapter Three

Greig glanced nervously around the hospital room as the obstetrician examined his wife. He had attended every appointment with Lisa during the pregnancy, but he couldn't help but feel out of place during some of the more intimate examinations. The sound of the doctor removing her latex gloves snapped him back to attention.

While Greig had initially thought the hippie doctor to be a little on the kooky side, he had grown to like her a lot in the time that Lisa had been in her care. He watched as Dr. Collins tossed the gloves into the trash and pumped a dollop of hand sanitizer out of the bottle by the bedside.

"What's the verdict, doctor?" Lisa asked nervously.

"Everything is as it should be, so you can relax. You are four centimeters dilated, and your boy is in the exact position he should be."

"How soon before delivery?" Greig asked, a flush rising to his cheeks.

"Tough to say, papa bear," Dr. Collins said. "We can move things along by getting mama here to walk around." The doctor placed a hand on Lisa's belly. "How's the pain level?"

"Not bad at all. It ramps up when the contractions hit, but it's manageable for now."

"That's good. I'm going to be here most of the night, and I'll check in on you regularly. If the pain gets too hot to handle, you let me know, and we'll get you set up with an epidural."

Lisa nodded and eased her body into the mountain of pillows at her back as Dr. Collins flashed her a wink and headed out of the room.

"What do you want to do, love? Do you want to rest up a bit or take a little walk around the ward?"

With a groan, Lisa pushed herself up and said, "I suppose I should follow doctor's orders.

Would you care to escort me around the block, good sir?"

They moved out into the maternity ward's long corridor and slowly started heading towards the windows at the far end. Greig held his wife's hand as she held onto the wall railing with the other, slowly waddling across the shiny floor, the soles of her house slippers squeaking on the polished surface with each step. They paused every ten minutes or so as the contractions hit, causing Lisa to bend over, hand on belly, as she exhaled short, little breaths.

Greig offered words of encouragement, telling her how great she was doing, but he could tell that she was becoming annoyed with his constant fawning, so he quickly changed his tune. "So, we probably need to make a final decision on the name."

They reached the end of the hallway, and Lisa pointed to a comfortable looking recliner that sat by the window. She let out a huge sigh of contentment the moment her behind hit the padded cushion. "Which way are you leaning?" she finally asked.

"I'm torn, to be honest. I mean, I like Graham, but is it too much with the G names, what with my old man being a Gary?"

Lisa laughed and then sucked in her breath as another contraction hit. She quickly moved into her breathing exercises and let out a long exhale as it passed. "I can just hear it now. Hey, Grandpa Gary, Greig and Graham are here. It has a poetic ring to it," she teased.

"It sounds worse than I imagined."

"I'm kidding, babe. I like Graham a lot. I've secretly been calling him that at home already, so it might be too late to change."

"I see who wears the trousers in this household," Greig laughed.

"Yes, and how sexy are those stretchy maternity jeans?"

"You make anything look good," Greig said as he helped his wife back to her feet. Are you ready for the trek back to your room? Maybe we could stop at the vending machine and pick up supplies in case we need to camp out halfway."

Lisa flashed a look of mock disgust but then raised her eyebrows as a thought struck. "You don't think they have gummy bears in there, do you?"

"Tell you what. Let's get you back to bed, and then I'll go track some of those jelly bastards down."

"I knew there was a reason I kept you around," Lisa joked, poking Greig in the side with her elbow.

***

Afternoon passed slowly into the evening before drifting into the early hours of the morning. With each passing hour, the maternity ward grew quieter and a little darker, as the lights were steadily dimmed to match the color of the sky.

Greig tried to read by the low light while Lisa slept. Dr. Collins had been in and out all day, letting them both know that they might be in this one for the long haul. Her shift was now over, but she had promised to return in the morning to assess the situation.

Kissing his wife softly on the forehead, Greig leaned back in the chair by the bed and closed his eyes for what felt like a moment. When he opened them again, he squinted against the bright daylight blasting in through the blinds. He struggled to focus for a moment, but once he got his bearings, he noticed a hive of activity in the room, all of it orchestrated by Dr. Collins.

"Good morning, sleepyhead," Lisa said, throwing a pillow at her husband.

"What did I miss?" he replied, as a young nurse pushed a cart past him and out of the room.

"My epidural is in, and I'm on a medication that should help speed things up. I will, though, miss our walks."

"Very funny. What's the medication."

Dr. Collins fiddled with an IV bag and turned to face Greig. "It's called Picotin. Lisa should be further along than she is now, so we are going to try this, but I'm not waiting much longer before scheduling a C-section."

"Is the baby okay?" Greig asked, a knot forming in his belly.

"Your boy is fine. It's time to get him out, though. I have a theater getting prepped as we speak. I'm giving it two more hours tops, and then we move." The doctor glanced at her watch, gave the IV bag another squeeze, and then slipped out of the room.

"I'm sorry I slept through all that," Greig said. "How are you holding up?"

"I'm feeling no pain at all. That epidural is some voodoo magic."

Reaching out, Greig took his wife's hands in his own. 'I'm so proud of you. I wish we had done this sooner, and I'm sorry I made you wait. I know how badly you wanted a baby."

"You have no reason to apologize, Mr. Ramsay. You have worked so hard to make a nice life for us. The timing is perfect, and I'm proud of you."

Greig turned his head and lay on Lisa's belly, trying his best to hold back the happy tears that were threatening to break free. A single tear forced its way out as his wife ran her fingers through his dark, wavy hair. "How did I get so lucky?"

"We both did. Our boy is going to be the luckiest of all. He will be so, so loved, but I think it's time you teach him our song."

"How do I do that?"

"You're right where he can hear you. Just sing."

He felt a little self-conscious at first, but Greig slowly began to sing. "Your love is all I need, baby, you're the best for me. Come and rock my dreams but take the chance for me. You're the best thing that ever happened to me or my world. You're the best thing that ever happened, so don't go away."

Lisa began to join in, singing softly as she continued to play with Greig's hair. They stayed that way until Dr. Collins strode into the room wearing surgical scrubs.

"Okay, mama bear, let's get you into surgery and bring your little man into the world."

Chapter Four

Greig stood in an exterior space beyond the operating room, watching through the two-way glass as Dr. Collins and her team prepped Lisa for the C-section. A nurse helped him get into a set of scrubs as she went over the delivery room rules.

"Talk to your wife all you want, but do not try to engage with the doctor, the anesthetist, or any of the other medical professionals in the delivery room, got it?"

"Yes, ma'am."

"You are not going to see much, as we will keep you at the opposite end of the table, right by your wife's head. That said, if you feel yourself getting queasy, raise your hand, and we will get you out of there. We'll have enough going on without having to worry about you passing out on us."

Greig nodded as the nurse placed a surgical cap on his head and handed him a mask and a pair of booties.

"Get those on, and I will take you in. It looks as though they are about ready to start."

Fumbling with the mask, Greig finally managed to steady his shaking hands enough to put it in place. He slipped the booties over his shoes, nodded again, and followed the nurse into the delivery room. She steered him to a wheeled chair sitting at the head of the operating table. If the doctors and nurses saw him coming in, they gave no indication, going about their business as though he were invisible.

Lisa turned to face him and presented him with a glassy-eyed smile, raising her left hand, which he took and gave a squeeze.

The doctor mumbled something to the anesthetist that Greig didn't quite catch before she flashed the thumbs-up sign and said, "Okay, Lisa. Here we go. You are going to feel a little bit of pressure in your abdomen, which is perfectly normal."

A small cloth screen blocked Greig's view of the proceedings, so he instead turned all his attention to his wife. A thin patina of sweat broke out on her forehead as her pale skin flushed at the cheekbones. The grip on his hand grew a little tighter, her nails digging into his flesh. Greig grinned and leaned forward, singing into her ear. "You're the best thing that ever happened to me or my world."

The sounds of the delivery room melted into the distance, the sound of his wife's breathing and his singing all that he heard until he heard Dr. Collins say, "You have a healthy baby boy."

He watched as a nurse took the baby over to a smaller table across the room, a bright light shining down on the metallic surface. The nurse cleaned off the little one and used a suction device to clear some gunk away from his nose and mouth. Once it was clear, an ear-splitting wail echoed around the room. The nurse swaddled the baby in a blanket and brought him over to the operating table, placing him on Lisa's chest.

"Congratulations, Mom and Dad."

The antiseptic scent of the delivery room was no match for the smell of a newborn baby. They both breathed it in as they smothered the still bawling child with kisses. "Welcome to the world, wee man, Greig managed between sobs.

As he leaned in to kiss his wife, Greig noticed that the color had drained from her face. The usual sparkle coming from her blue eyes had vanished, replaced by a dull shade the color of an untended swimming pool.

The last thing he heard before the nurse took Graham and whisked Greig out of the delivery room while he was still seated in the chair was Dr. Collins saying, "We need to stop the bleeding now."

***

Greig sat in the waiting room, the surgical cap and mask gripped tightly in his hands. He had never felt more alone or afraid in his life, and while his relationship with Lisa's parents was icy at best, he wished that they would show up soon. They had been at a company function when he called and said that it would be bad manners to leave before they had dessert. It seemed that Greig had not done enough to explain the gravity of the situation, but the reality was that Tim and Martha Chambers cared little about anything other than themselves and how their rich friends viewed them.

The clock on the wall ticked ever so slowly, the second hand seeming to force itself through some viscous fluid embedded in the timepiece. After what seemed like an eternity, the door to the waiting room opened, and Dr. Collins stepped inside, head down, scrubs covered in red smears that made the pale green outfit look like a Jackson Pollock design.

Greig leaped to his feet and rushed the doctor, grabbing her by the shoulders. "How is Lisa doing? Can I see her?"

She removed his hands from her shoulders and steered Greig back to the chairs, sitting down beside him and taking his hand. "Greig, I am so sorry. We tried our best, but I'm afraid to say that Lisa has passed."

Eyes wide, Greig stammered, "What…how can…what?"

The doctor began to talk, but Greig heard nothing but snippets about uterine cramping, hemorrhaging, and a host of other medical terms that meant nothing to him.

"GREIG."

He snapped back to reality to see Dr. Collins leaning in close, a hand on his shoulder. "Can I see her?"

"As soon as we get her cleaned up and presentable, I promise. Do you want to see your boy? He's beautiful."

Greig nodded, choking back the tears, all of which came loose in a torrent when the nurse handed over his son.

"I'll be back in a few minutes when she's ready," Dr. Collins said.

Reaching down, Greig adjusted the blue wool hat on his boy's head, revealing a little tuft of blond hair that looked just like Lisa's. The pain in Greig's heart was almost unbearable, but he held it together as he cradled his son in his arms.

He looked so tiny in Greig's hands, so in need of protection. A piercing scream sounded from beyond the waiting room door, the unmistakable sound of Martha Chambers receiving the news about her daughter.

Lifting his son to his shoulder, hand on his head for support, Greig whispered, "It's just you and me, wee man. It's just you and me."

Chapter Five

13 Years Later

Greig logged out of the Zoom meeting and closed down his laptop, quickly tidying up the mess he had made in his home office. Peeking out through the bay window, he looked toward the end of the street, hoping he had finished work before the school bus arrived. The street remained kid-free, so he slipped on a pair of runners, grabbed his coffee, and stepped outside onto the front steps of his house.

His knees popped as he sat on the top step, soaking up the rays of a glorious spring day in the south. He could feel the sun on his head, the rays nipping at the ever-expanding area of exposed skin at the back. Greig had toyed with the idea of shaving his head completely when he first noticed the bald spot, but it had yet to reach the ridiculous comb-over stage, so he had held off. Plus, he liked the salt and pepper look that he was rocking in his remaining locks.

He thought about his dad, as he often did when the subject of his hair came around. His old man had gone bald very early and had not done so gracefully, relying on creative styling and some shoe polish-type substance for the barer patches. Even now, the hair that remained on Gary Ramsay's head looked like a garden left to rot, the tufts sprouting from his ears much like weeds.

Turning on the camera on his phone, Greig tried to position it so that he could see the back of his head on the screen. It was impossible to get a decent look, so he pulled the phone down to face level and examined himself. Small bags were beginning to form under his green eyes, and crow's feet spread out from the sides, but overall he looked good for a man in his mid-forties. Not that any of it really mattered to Greig. Other than a couple of dates here and there, a serious relationship had never emerged since Lisa passed. He did feel lonely at times, but his boy and his work, in that order, were all that mattered.

As he sipped at his coffee, the sound of squealing brakes filled the air as the school bus rolled to a stop at the end of the street. Greig had to force himself not to go down there and meet his son, as the boy had claimed independence at thirteen, saying that it was embarrassing to have his dad meet him at the bus when he was a teenager. It was a demand that Greig willingly accepted after seeing Graham get into the habit of jogging the final few yards, a lopsided smile spread across his face when he spotted his dad sitting on the steps.

Greig waited for that moment, but it never came. Graham trudged up the street, head down, his backpack hanging loosely in his right hand, the bottom mere inches off the sidewalk.

His brow creased in concern, Greig stood and moved to the bottom of the stairs, waiting for Graham to take the final few steps, which he did even more slowly than the rest of his walk. "You okay there, kiddo?"

The boy looked up and forced a smile. "Just tired, dad."

"Another rough night?"

"Yeah."

"If you want, we can skip soccer practice tonight."

Graham recoiled at the statement. "Heck, no. How am I ever going to play for Scotland if I start skipping practices?"

"How is anyone on your team going to understand that southern drawl," Greig said, tousling the boy's blond hair.

"I understand you just fine, so I don't imagine it would be that hard," Graham said with a smirk.

"Get in that house, you cheeky monkey." Greig followed his son inside, closing the door behind him. "Any homework you need to take care of?"

41

"Nope." Graham placed his pack on the hook behind the door and blew a kiss at the picture of his mom that hung on the wall. It was a daily routine, but one that brought a lump to Greig's throat every single time.

"Okay, good. We have a couple of hours before we need to go to practice. Go try and get a nap, and I'll make something to eat. What do you fancy?"

"I'm not really hungry. Maybe just a sandwich."

Greig watched his son head upstairs, his legs looking as though they were getting heavier with each step. Graham had been tired and lacking in his usual energy for a couple of weeks, but this was his worse day yet. If things were the same tomorrow, a trip to the doctor's office might need to be the next step.

Trying to put Graham's sluggishness out of mind, Greig moved around the house, tidying up areas that didn't need it. He had a housekeeper come in a couple of times a week to tidy up and prep meals for a few days, but it was an easy job for her. Greig has always been house proud and took the time to ensure that things were as neat and orderly as he could make them.

After about an hour of aimless chores, he put together a couple of peanut butter and jelly sandwiches and poured a large glass of milk. Heading upstairs, he knocked gently on Graham's bedroom door and stepped inside. It was the typical teenager's room, with dirty clothes lying everywhere except in the laundry hamper in the corner. The desk on the far wall was piled high with textbooks that surrounded an open laptop displaying a Manchester United screensaver. Posters of soccer players and video game characters plastered the walls, covering the childish cartoon wallpaper that Greig had never got around to changing.

The curtains were closed, the room bathed in the dull glow of a soccer ball shaped nightlight plugged into the wall. The boy lay buried under the covers, his blond locks the only thing visible from the door. Greig crept in, keeping an eye out for stray toys on the floor, and placed the sandwiches and milk on the bedside table. Graham groaned and rolled over, pulling himself into a fetal position, when Greig gave him a gentle waking nudge.

Reaching over, Greigh placed a hand on his son's forehead and was shocked to feel him burning up. He headed into the attached bathroom and ran a washcloth under the cold tap. Wringing out the excess water, he returned to the bedroom and wiped his boy's face with the cloth before folding it over and placing it on his forehead.

Greig reached into his pocket and called Evan Hunt, his best friend and assistant coach on the soccer team. Evan answered on the second ring. "Hey Evan, it's Greig. How're things?"

"Not too shabby, pal. What can I do you for?"

"I've got a bit of a favor to ask. Graham is running a fever and won't be at practice tonight, which means I won't be either. Can you take care of it tonight?"

"Of course. Megan and I can come over later if you like. Do you need anything?"

Evan and Megan had been his primary support system after Lisa passed, with Megan playing the role of a personal chef and surrogate mom for the first few months. It has taken that long for Greig to manage his grief and start behaving like the father that his boy needed. "I'm good, Evan. I'm going to let him sleep and try to get an appointment with the doctor as soon as possible. He hasn't been himself for a couple of weeks now."

"Poor kid. I'll tell you what, Megan is friendly with the receptionist at the doctor's office. I'll ask her to give them a call and see if they can squeeze you in first thing in the morning."

"That would be a huge help, mate."

"On it now. I'll call you back in a couple of minutes."

Grieg sat on the bed, hanging up the call, and wiped the washcloth over Graham's face again. The boy's T-shirt was damp from sweat, but he didn't want to fuss with him too much, so he let it be.

Realizing that he was hungry, Greig grabbed one of the sandwiches and took a bite. He was not a huge fan of peanut butter, but the jelly's sweet notes made him happy. As he chugged down the milk, his phone began to vibrate. Thumbing the speaker button, he held the phone to his ear. "Hello."

"Greig. Megan here. How is Graham feeling?"

"He's out like a light and running a fever."

"Bless his heart. I talked to Sharon at Dr. Carpenter's office and called in a favor. The doctor will see Graham at nine in the morning."

"You are a star, Megan."

"Anything for that sweet boy of yours. Do you want me to whip up some soup in case he wakes up hungry later? I'll get Evan to drive it over."

"No, thank you. He hasn't had much of an appetite of late."

"Well, you be sure to call if you need anything. We are always here for you."

Greig swallowed hard and cleared his throat. "Thanks, Megan. I'm not sure what I would do without you."

After saying their goodbyes, Greig ran to his bedroom and brought over a chair that he sat beside Graham's bed. Plugging his phone into the charger, he set it on the bedside table and then took one more trip to pick up the book he was currently reading. Flipping over the front cover, Greigh sat and stretched out his legs so that they were resting on his son's bed. He had a feeling it was going to be a sleepless night.

Chapter Six

They arrived at the doctor's office early. They were immediately whisked into an examination room, which came as a surprise to Greig, who was used to waiting up to an hour beyond his appointment time when he had visited Dr. Carpneter in the past, either alone or with Graham.

Waking up Graham had been a bit of a chore that morning, and while his fever appeared to have abated, he had balked at the idea of eating anything for breakfast. Greig had managed to get his son to accept a glass of orange juice, but he had sipped a little and pushed it away to make space to rest his head on the dining room table.

Greig had his arm around his son's shoulders, the boy's head buried in his chest, when the doctor stepped into the room, clipboard in hand.

"Good morning, gentlemen. How are we today?" the elderly doctor asked cheerily.

"I'm good, thank you, but my lad here is a bit under the weather."

The doctor scanned the paper on his clipboard and said, "Sharon tells me he's running a fever. What other symptoms are we looking at?"

"Well, he's been a little lethargic of late and hasn't had much of an appetite."

"A couple of weeks or so."

Dr. Carpenter scribbled some notes as Greig spoke and then said, "Can you hop up on the table for me, Graham, so that I can have a look."

Shuffling across the examination room like a zombie, Graham climbed onto the table and sat on the edge, the tissue paper below him crinkling as he moved to find a comfortable spot.

The doctor removed an ear thermometer from a mount on the wall, slipped a plastic cover on the end, and inserted it into Graham's ear. The thermometer beeped, and the doctor took note of the temperature. "A little on the high side."

"He's definitely not as bad as he was last night," Greig chimed in.

"Can you lift your shirt for me, please, Graham?" Carpenter said, removing a stethoscope from around his neck and pressing it against the boy's chest. He moved the device around slowly before removing it from his ears and placing it back around his neck. "Did he have any other flu-like symptoms besides the fever?"

"Just the ones I mentioned."

The doctor nodded and began to examine Graham's neck, pressing down on different areas. The boy winced at one tender spot. "Does that hurt?"

"Yes," Graham said meekly.

"Well, his lymph nodes are swollen, which could be a sign of many different things, most of which are relatively benign. I'm going to prescribe some antibiotics, which should help with the swelling. I will, though, want to see him back here in a week. You can make an appointment with Sharon on the way out."

"Thank you, Dr. Carpenter," Greig said.

"Not a problem. I hope you feel better soon, Graham. I think Sharon might have a lollipop out at the reception desk. All the colors of the rainbow. I bet she'll give you one."

They headed out to the reception area, where Sharon was ready with the prescription and the lollipop, which Graham stuffed in his pants pocket with a hastily mumbled thank you. They made the appointment for the following week and then stepped out into the sunshine, just as the clock in the city hall tower chimed the half-hour.

"Are you hungry yet, wee man?"

"No, but I sure am tired again."

"Okay, back home to bed then. I think we should keep you home from school for the rest of the week.:

Graham nodded. "Dad?"

"What's up?"

"I don't mean to sound like a baby, but can you carry me to the car?"

Greig dropped to his haunches and said, "All aboard the Flying Scotsman. Next stop, Lawrenceton Estates."

The boy clambered onto Greig's back and draped his arms around his neck. Reaching down, Greig scooped under his son's knees to get him into the piggyback position, suddenly concerned that the boy felt like a bag of bones. He could feel Graham's ribs poking into his back, and while the kid had always been tall and lean, this felt somehow different.

As they walked up the street to the parking deck, they passed several posters showing the image of a missing local girl named Kayleigh Barnes. Greig wondered how her parents must be feeling and began to think about how he would cope if anything were seriously wrong with his son. He tried to push the thought aside, but it gnawed at his insides, ripping and tearing like a rabid dog.

***

Over the next couple of days, Graham began to show some signs of improvement, but by day three, the fever was back, accompanied by bouts of vomiting. Greig called the doctor's office to see if they could move up the appointment they had made, with Sharon happy to oblige. After a more thorough examination, Dr. Carpenter took on a serious expression.

"Okay, Mr. Ramsay, I would like to send Graham for a few more tests."

A wave of nausea washed over Greig, but he swallowed hard and managed to speak. "What do you think the problem is?"

The doctor sighed heavily and cast a sideways glance at Graham, who lay on the examination table snoring quietly. "Might I ask if there is a history of cancer in your family?"

"Not on my side, but my wife's parents both died of cancer, a couple of years apart. Are you telling me that my boy has cancer?"

"I won't know for sure until we run more tests, but the lymph nodes in his armpits, as well as in his neck, are swollen. That, combined with his other symptoms, suggests that we might be looking at Hodgkin's lymphoma."

Greig laced his fingers around the back of his head and squeezed tight in an effort to stop the room from spinning. "When...I mean, how will we know for sure?"

"The first order of business would be to have some blood work done, which I can make happen today. If the blood samples show signs of infection, usually originating in the liver or spleen, then we will need a biopsy of the swollen lymph nodes. That will give us a definitive answer."

"If it's lymphoma, then what?"

"Let's take one step at a time, Mr. Ramsay. It shouldn't take more than a day or two to get the blood test results back. I'm also going to schedule the biopsy appointment for early next week. We can cancel that if the tests come back negative. I want all our ducks in a row if we do need to deal with the worst-case scenario."

The rest of the day took place in a fog, as Greig tried to remain upbeat in front of his son, who sat through the blood tests like a champ. A couple of days later, when the call came in from the doctor's office to inform him that the biopsy would be required, Greig decided it was time to talk with his son.

Graham sat propped up in bed, laptop on his legs as he worked through some school assignments. Greig sat down on the end of the bed and flashed his son a smile that felt utterly phony.

"What's up, Dad?" Graham asked, peeking over the top of his laptop.

"You got a minute to talk to your old man?"

"Sure thing."

Greig suddenly noticed how gaunt his son looked with the laptop set aside and the glow from the screen removed. His cheekbones stuck out a little more than usual. And dark circles ringed his eyes. "How are you feeling today?" Greig asked.

"About the same."

Heart hammering, Greig said, "About that. I heard back from Dr. Carpenter today. He called about your blood tests."

The boy stared at him through eyes the color of Lisa's, no sign of fear on display.

"Anyway, they now need to do another test called a biopsy, which will help them figure out why you feel the way you do. Once they do that, they will know how to fix it."

"I know that word."

"Which one?"

"Biopsy. I remember hearing you mention it when Grandma Martha was sick."

Greig squirmed and tried to think how to proceed. "That's right. You have some memory, kid. No wonder you do so well in school."

"I'm not scared, Dad. You shouldn't be either."

"I don't want to be, but I love you and don't like when you are sick."

Graham stared at his father for a moment and then spoke quietly. "Every day, I blow a little kiss to Mom, but I also wish I could hug her. I wish I could talk to her. If they can't fix me, I'll finally get to do that."

Greig wanted to run, wanted to head outside and scream and break apart. Instead, he gripped the comforter with his left hand and patted his son's leg with his right. "That's a great way to think about it. Is it selfish that I want you here with me?"

Graham tilted his head to the side and said, "Nah, I'm the coolest kid you know."

"You got that right. Now, get over here and give your old man a hug."

He pulled the boy in tight and fought back the tears. If his boy could be so brave, he needed to find a way to be the same.

Chapter Seven

Lost in thought, Greig almost let out a little scream when Sharon called his name in the waiting room. He and Graham followed her through to the examination room that had become something of a second home over the past couple of weeks. They sat on the hard plastic chairs and held hands as they waited for the doctor.

"What color of lollipop are you planning on nabbing this time?" Greig asked.

"Red, definitely red. Cherry is the bomb."

"You know, I think you go get those suckers because you have a crush on Sharon. She is pretty cute."

Graham's face flushed, and he pulled his hand away from his dad. "Gross. She's ancient."

"She's younger than I am," Greig fired back.

"You are the Crypt Keeper," Graham said, trying to stifle a giggle.

"That's quite enough out of you, young man." Greig tried to maintain a serious face, but as soon as he saw his son's shoulders bobbing up and down in an effort not to laugh, he lost it. The pair of them were still laughing and wiping away tears when Dr. Carpenter knocked on the door and stepped inside, instantly turning the atmosphere somber.

The doctor usually engaged in small talk, but, today, he was all business. "Good to see you both again," he said, looking down at the papers attached to his trusty clipboard. "I wish I had better news for you today, but I'm afraid I don't."

Reaching out, Greig found his son's hand again.

"Would you like to stay and listen, Graham, or would you rather sit out front with Sharon?"

The boy flushed again as he spoke. "I want to stay here with my dad."

"We have been talking about what might happen here today," Greig said. "We are prepared."

Dr. Carpenter nodded. "Very well. The biopsy results show that Graham has stage four Hodgkin's lymphoma, so it is imperative that we start with treatment immediately. We would…"

Greig raised his hand to interrupt the doctor. "Hold on. Stage four? He's only had symptoms for a few weeks."

"Yes. The swollen lymph nodes are often painless, so it's easy to mistake the other symptoms, when they do arrive, as something else entirely."

"What now?" Greig asked, beginning to feel frantic.

"We would like to start chemotherapy and radiation treatments as soon as possible. The positive aspect here is Graham's age. Kids can handle larger doses than adults, so we can attack this quite aggressively."

Graham raised his hand.

"Yes?" Carpenter said.

"What if I didn't do the treatments?"

"That is not something I would recommend. You are young and strong, and while you wouldn't feel very good during the chemotherapy, it could potentially make you feel better."

"Let's stop for a moment, please," Greig said. "What are the chances of the chemo being successful."

Dr. Carpenter cleared his throat and studied his notes for a moment. "Realistically, given the late stage of the lymphoma, twenty-five to thirty percent would be the best-case scenario."

"What if I didn't do the treatments?" Graham asked a little more forcefully.

"You would have good days and bad, and even a few where you didn't feel sick at all, but…"

"I would die."

The doctor glanced over at Greig, who was staring off into space, his mouth hanging open. "Mr. Ramsay."

"What? Oh, yes, tell us, please."

"I don't like to put time limits on things, but I would guess about six weeks or so." His voice trailed off as he spoke, the delivery of bad news never getting any easier, no matter how many times he did it.

Greig nodded assertively as he came to a decision. "When can we…"

"I don't want it," Graham interrupted.

"This is up to your father, I'm afraid," Dr. Carpenter said.

Turning to face his son, Greig asked, "Why wouldn't you want to do it?"

"I remember something else Grandma Martha said. Something about how Grandpa was sick and how he had no…" He chewed on his bottom lip as he thought of the phrase. "Quality, something about quality."

"Quality of life," Greig and the doctor said in unison.

"Yeah, that's it. I don't want to take medicine and feel sick all the time and have my hair fall out. That's not cool. I want some good days with my dad."

The doctor nodded and looked at Greig. "Do you need a moment to make a decision?"

Greig looked at his son and imagined life without him. Losing Lisa had been tough enough, but losing his boy, too, his last link to his wife. Was that something he could handle? His voice cracked as he spoke. "Are you positive that's what you want?"

"I am, Dad, but I also want one more thing."

***

The first few hours home after the doctor's office were a flurry of activity. Graham hung out with Megan and watched movies while Greig got to work in his office. The first order of business was a Zoom meeting with the top brass at his company, where he let them know the situation with his son and that he would be out for the foreseeable future.

After a round of sympathetic messages from the troops, Greig spoke one on one with Timothy Allen, his second in command, letting him know that he was in charge for the time being.

The next stop was a travel website, where he booked flights, a hotel, and a car rental, the latter of which made him nervous. Greig was a confident driver, but he prayed that he would remember to drive on the other side of the road when the time came.

Next up was a Facebook group text with his friends back home. They were all saddened by the news about Graham but also excited at the prospect of seeing their friend again. They were also all aware that finding tickets for the upcoming Scotland versus England football match was at the top of the list. Malcolm Crossan, Greig's best friend from back in the day, promised to do everything, legal and otherwise, to secure the tickets.

The last call of the day was the one he dreaded the most. Opening up the Skype app on his laptop, Greig went through his contact list and clicked on his mum and dad's listing. The familiar Skype tune played as the call attempted to connect. Just as he was about to give up, his father's face appeared on the screen, hair flying in all directions as usual.

"How's it going, son? Good to see you."

"I'm good, dad. Is mum around? I have some news to share."

"Hold on." Gary Ramsay turned away from the screen, the overhead light shining on his bald head, giving Greig a glimpse of his future. "LORNA, YOUR BOY IS ON THE COMPUTER PHONE. SAYS HE HAS NEWS."

Greig could faintly hear his mum in the background, her voice growing louder as she got closer. "I'm not bloody deaf, you old bugger. No need to yell at me."

"I was not yelling."

"Aye, you were. Budge over, so I can see my son."

Gary moved sideways, allowing Lorna to squeeze in beside him, half of each of their faces taking up the entire screen.

"If you move back a wee bit, I'll be able to see you both," Greig said, going through the same routine he did on every Skype call. His parents fidgeted and fussed but eventually got themselves into a position where they were both fully visible.

"How's that?" Gary asked.

"Perfect. So, like I said, I have a couple of pieces of news."

"Good or bad?" Lorna asked, looking over the rim of her glasses.

"Both. I'll start with the bad." Greig took some time to recount the past couple of weeks' events, holding it together even as he watched his parents fall apart. His mum fished a tissue out from under the sleeve of her sweater and dabbed at her eyes while his dad disappeared for a moment, only to return with red-rimmed eyes and a generous portion of whiskey in a pint glass.

"The poor wee soul," Lorna sniffed. "Is he about?"

"He's watching a movie with one of my friends, and I don't want him seeing you both upset."

"I'm fine, son," Gary said, swallowing two fingers of whiskey before wiping his eyes and blaming the alcohol for making them water.

"Anyway, you'll see him soon enough. We are coming to visit in a couple of days."

Lorna let out a little squeal of delight and started crying again. "I'll get your old bedroom ready. There isn't much space in there, but we can squeeze you both in."

"Don't worry about me, mum. I'm happy on the couch."

"When are you flying in, son?" Gary asked, pulling a whiskey bottle into view and topping up his glass.

"We leave on Friday morning, but we won't be up to Kilbrennan until Monday or Tuesday. I want to show the wee man around Glasgow and take a surprise trip before we head your way."

Lorna nodded as she stared off into space, her lips moving like a ventriloquist dummy.

"Are you alright, Mum?"

"She's daft as a brush, Greig."

"Shut it, you," Lorna said, digging her husband in the side with her elbow. "I'm putting a plan together. I need to get some food in, get the laundry started, and have your lazy bastard of a father move my knitting stuff out of your room and into the garden shed."

"Mum, you have six days to get it all done. Relax."

"I'll relax when I'm d...Oh, sorry, son. What a thing to say." Pulling the tissue out again, she leaped out of the chair and scurried out of the room, waving as she went.

Gary slid his chair across and sat in the center of the screen again. "She'll be alright. We all will. We look forward to seeing you next week, son. It's been too long."

"It has indeed, Dad. I'll see you then."

The conversation ended as awkwardly as always, with neither of them willing to commit to an "I love you" on the way out. Those types of platitudes were reserved for the pub or house parties where the alcohol flowed freely, and inhibitions weren't locked up quite so tight.

Closing up the laptop, Greig headed into the living room, where Megan and Graham sat cozied up under a blanket on the couch watching *Iron Man*. He stood and watched them, imagining for a moment that Lisa was still alive and that she was the one on the sofa with their boy. "We are all set," he finally said, pulling himself out of the daydream.

Graham threw the blanket aside and turned to face his dad, a beaming smile on his face. "You did it?" he asked.

"I did. We are going to Scotland." He moved over to the sofa and lifted his son over his head, the boy spreading his arms and making airplane sounds.

"Scooooooootland, woohoo."

Chapter Eight

The plane broke through the clouds, opening up to green fields stretching as far as the eye could see. As they drifted ever closer to the ground, fields and farmhouses gave way to small towns that looked like scale models seen from above.

Graham pressed his nose to the window and looked back and forth, as though watching a tennis match. "Do you think we flew over where Nana and Grankie live?" he asked without turning.

Greig smiled at his son using Grankie in place of Grandpa. The official title had come after overhearing Lorna call Gary a cranky old bastard on a video chat. Graham had pointed at the screen and said Grankie and the name had stuck ever since. "We might have, but we are well past it now." Leaning over his son's shoulder, Greig looked out the window and said, "We are flying over Glasgow now."

The plane glided slowly over the city, sinking ever lower until it touched the runway with a thump, the roar of the engines slowing down echoing through the cabin. Once they were at the gate, Greig allowed the majority of the passengers to leave before standing and getting their carry-on luggage out of the overhead compartment. "Are you ready to roll, wee man?"

Graham nodded excitedly and followed his dad down the aisle and out onto the jetway. Following the signs, they made their way to the luggage carousel, got their stuff, and headed through customs without a hitch. A visit to the rental car counter and a short bus ride to the car park later, they bundled into their vehicle and headed for the M8 motorway.

Greig was nervous at first, internally repeating the mantra of "keep left, keep left" until he finally relaxed. The roads were busy, but nothing compared to what he encountered in Atlanta. Following the GPS directions, they made it to their hotel in a little over a half-hour, where Greig breathed a sigh of relief when he handed the car keys over to the valet.

The room was even better than it looked on the website, the large window offering great views of the River Clyde and the Clyde Arc Bridge, which looked stunning all lit up at night. Greig was worried that Graham might be tired, but the boy was a bundle of energy. "Are you hungry, kiddo?"

"I am. Can we get fish and chips?"

"We can indeed. Let's go down to the lobby and find out if there's a chippy nearby."

"A chippy?"

"That's what we call a fish and chip shop. Just wait until you taste Irn-Bru. You are in for a treat."

The concierge directed them to a chip shop a short walk from the hotel. They sat on a bench outside and ate, the smell of vinegar tickling their noses. Graham let out a gasp as he took a swig of

Irn-Bru from the bottle. "You were right, Dad. This is so much better than Coca-cola."

After eating, they walked a little further, peering in shop windows, all of which were closed for the night. Greig noticed that Graham was beginning to slow down, so he picked him up and put him on his shoulders as they headed back to the hotel. "Let's get some sleep. We have an early start tomorrow."

"Where are we going?"

"You'll find out soon enough."

***

Greig felt terrible about waking his son up so early, but Graham hopped out of bed and into the shower without any complaints. "Well, that was easy," Greig muttered as he turned on the coffee maker.

After packing a small backpack with a few snacks and essentials, they took the elevator down to the lobby and headed out to the front of the hotel. A pair of black cabs sat by the entrance, diesel engines idling. Opening the door to the nearest of the two vehicles, Greig helped his boy inside and then slid in beside him.

"This is the coolest car ever," Graham gasped. 'It's like an old stagecoach.

'Let's hope we don't encounter any bandits on the trip," the driver called out from the front seat. "Where are you visiting from?"

"We just flew in from Atlanta last night," Greig said. "I was born and raised up north, but this is my boy's first visit since he was little."

"Ah, the brilliant. A wee father/son trip."

"It's my farewell tour," Graham said.

"How does that work then?" the driver asked, turning to face them.

Greig held up his hands and said, "Sorry about that. He's, well, he's sick, and this is where he wanted to come for a trip."

"You picked a fine place. My name is Jimmy. What should I call you boys?"

"I'm Graham, and this is my dad, Greig."

Removing his flat cap, Jimmy gave a little bow and said, "It will be my pleasure to be your driver. Where are we off to?"

"Central Station, please?"

"Right. Do you have a train to catch?" Jimmy asked, reaching over to turn on the meter.

"No set time. We are going to wing it."

Jimmy looked at Graham and asked, "Do you like football?"

"I love it, Jimmy. I play striker, or I did until I got sick. My dad is the coach, and I'm the top scorer."

"Who's your favorite team?"

"Manchester United, but Scotland is my number one."

Turning off the meter, Jimmy drummed his fingers against his chin. "If it's okay with your dad,

I could take you on a detour before we go to the train station. Maybe see some of the sights."

"What do you think, wee man? Are you up for an adventure?"

"Drive on, James," Greig said, trying his best to do a posh English accent.

Jimmy threw back his head and roared with laughter. "Let's do it."

For the next hour, they drove through the city, with Jimmy slowing down to point out buildings and statues, talking loudly to drown out the sound of blaring horns from the vehicles stuck behind him.

"Now, our final spot on the trip is right up ahead," Jimmy said, pointing out the front window.

Graham craned his neck to try and get a better look. It took a moment, but when he caught sight of the stadium, his jaw went slack as he let out a gasp. "Is that what I think it is?"

"If you think it's the famous Hampden Park, home of the Scotland National Team, then you would be correct, my good sir.

Traffic cones blocked the entrance to the parking lot outside the stadium, but Jimmy got as close as he could, pulling off the main road and turning the cab so that the stadium was on Graham's side.

"Have you been inside, Jimmy?" Graham asked.

"Many times. What about you, Greig?"

"Yes. Lots of good memories in there."

They sat in silence for a couple of minutes, staring at the stadium, each lost in their thoughts. "Are you going to the England game, Jimmy?"

"I'd like to, but the tickets are impossible to get. They sold out quickly. It'll be on the telly, though, so I'll take the night off and watch it."

As they pulled back into traffic and headed toward the city center, Graham placed his hand against the window as though trying to reach out and touch the stadium. Once it was out of sight, he went quiet and stared out the window.

The mood inside the cab was somber when Jimmy pulled into the taxi rank at the rear entrance to the station. The driver hopped out of the vehicle and opened the door on Graham's side. He helped the boy down then dropped to eye level, removing his cap and placing it under his arm. Holding out his hand, he said, "It was a pleasure being your chauffeur for the day. I hope you enjoy the rest of your trip.'

Pushing his hand aside, Graham moved in and threw his arms around the driver's neck, hugging him tightly. "Thank you, Jimmy. That was awesome."

As Graham moved aside, Greig moved in and shook Jimmy's hand, pressing a twenty-pound note into his palm. The driver looked at it for a moment and then shoved it into Greig's jacket pocket. "Your money is no good here. The pleasure was all mine. You both gave me a day I won't soon forget. You look after that lad, and look after yourself, too." With that, he turned, put his cap back on, and returned behind the wheel, waving out the window as he pulled away.

They watched until the cab was out of sight and then headed up the stairs leading to the train station. Once they reached the top, Greig felt a tug at his jacket. He turned to find Graham staring wide-eyed at the glass roof, the sunlight breaking through and glinting off the steel beams that ran across the massive open space.

"Pretty cool, eh?" Greig said.

"It's huge."

Pointing to a large display board off in the distance, Greig said, "That's where we see all the platform numbers and where the trains on each one are headed. Let's go and take a look."

They headed over to the board and scanned the destinations and departure times, some of which changes as trains departed and new ones arrived.

Graham studied the board, brow furrowed, as he tried to take it all in.

"Any destination jumping out at you?" Greig asked.

"Was it Edinburgh that you said had a castle in the middle of the street?"

"That's right."

The boy turned to face his dad, a serious look on his face. "Were you making that up?"

"There's only one way to know for sure." Greig put his arm around his son's shoulder and led him to the ticket booth, where they ordered a pair of return tickets to Edinburgh. Sitting on the train, they didn't have to wait long until it began to move, gliding slowly out of the station before picking up speed as it pulled free of Glasgow Central.

They were lucky enough to land on the express train, which meant there were no stops along the way. The train rattled along the tracks, the sound of its movement playing a constant rhythm that only changed when it passed through a tunnel.

"You know, when I was a wee boy, your grankie would take me on the train every now and again. I was scared of the sound it made, but my dad told me that it was just the train talking."

"What was it saying?"

It's saying it now if you really listen. I'll get you there, I'll get you there, I'll get you there."

Graham lowered his head as though trying to get his ears closer to the tracks. His body swayed side to side a little in time with the train, and then he sat up quickly and said, "That's exactly what it sounds like. That's awesome."

They watched as the countryside flew past until, about an hour after their journey began, the train started to slow down, brakes squealing loudly. It puttered along slowly as they passed through a green space that looked like a massive garden with flowers in bloom all over. Greig nudged his son and pointed up and out of the train window. Graham looked, went stiff as a board, and shouted, "It's real. You didn't make it up."

Right outside the window, looking close enough to touch, a towering rocky hillside rose up and dominated the skyline. Edinburgh Castle sat on top, its stone wall looking impenetrable as a Scottish flag fluttered in the wind on the highest turret.

"Do you want to go up there? It's a bit of a walk, but if we hustle, we'll get there in time for something special."

Graham frowned for a moment, looking a little concerned. "It's a long way up. I want to go, but I might need to hitch a piggyback ride part of the way."

"That can be arranged, "Greig said with a wink.

They left the train and hurried up Waverley Station's steps, which led to Princes Street, the city's main shopping thoroughfare. Graham held on to his father's jacket as they moved through the crowd and eventually onto a steep side street. They hadn't gone far when Greig picked up his boy and placed him on his shoulders. It was a longer, steeper climb than he remembered, but once they reached the top and arrived at the castle esplanade, he realized it was worth it.

The sprawling forecourt that served as the castle's entrance was a hive of activity, with countless tourists posing for pictures. Graham tapped his dad on the head, a sign that he wanted down to go exploring. They made their way across the esplanade and bought tickets to the castle, passing through the main gate and up a cobbled lane that led to the fortress's central area.

Greig looked at his watch and placed a hand on Graham's back. "We need to hurry; it's almost one o'clock. Can you manage?"

"I'm okay, Dad. What's happening at one?"

"You're going to love it."

They made their way to the far corner of the castle, where the view out across the city was breathtaking. Ignoring the view, Graham's eyes instead settled on a weapon that sat in front of a small windowed building. "Is that a cannon?" he whispered.

"That, wee man, is the Edinburgh Gun, but everyone calls it's the one o'clock gun."

Before Graham could ask why it got that name, a soldier in uniform emerged from the house. He wore a black uniform that sported a white belt and red stripes down his pants' side. His hat was pulled low, the brim keeping the top half of his face in shadow. He ignored the small crowd standing watching from behind the chained off area where the gun sat, marching over to the weapon and cranking a handle that raised the barrel to a forty-five-degree angle. Reaching into his pocket with a white-gloved hand, he removed a watch and studied the face.

"Is he going to fire that thing?" Graham asked, more than a little alarmed.

Before Greig could reply, the soldier reached out and fired the gun, right on the stroke of one o'clock. A loud boom tore through the sky, and a plume of white smoke rose from the gun barrel.

Graham looked out over the city, waiting to see one of Princes Street buildings collapse when the shell hit. He let out a sigh of relief when that didn't happen and joined in with the other visitors' applause watching the ceremony. "That was amazing. I've never seen a gun that big."

"You haven't seen anything yet. I know where they have an even bigger one."

They toured the remainder of the castle at their own pace, spending a lot of time at Mons Meg, a massive black cannon of which Graham was in awe. He demanded that his dad take several pictures, claiming that none of his friends would believe that a cannon of that size existed.

Once they covered every square inch of the castle, they made their way down the Royal Mile, picking up some souvenirs in the small shops that lined the street and stopping in at a pub for a rest and a bite to eat. By the time they reached Holyrood

Palace at the bottom of the Royal Mile, Graham looked out on his feet, his complexion pale. Greig flagged down a cab that took them back to the station and the train that led them back to Glasgow.

As he tucked his son under the covers in his hotel room bed, Graham's eyes flickered open for the briefest of moments. "That was an awesome day, Dad. What are we doing tomorrow?"

Greig leaned over and kissed his boy on the forehead. "I think we'll have a rest day tomorrow. Maybe just order in some room service and watch some movies. How does that sound?"

The boy nodded, a smile barely touching the corners of his mouth, and then he was asleep. Greig laid down on the bed and pressed the TV remote's power button, setting the sound just loud enough to hear. He blinked heavily as he watched a recap of the day's soccer games before he, too, fell asleep.

Chapter Nine

The decision to make Sunday a rest day proved to be a smart one. Graham awoke in the middle of the night crying for his father, sweat pouring off him in a tidal wave. Greig had managed to find an ice machine on their floor and had filled their ice bucket to brimming. Throughout the remainder of the night, he wrapped the ice in a washcloth and held it to his son's head and body, trying to bring down the fever with the aid of some children's Tylenol.

The fever broke early Sunday morning but returned with a vengeance later in the day, accompanied by a bout of vomiting that left Graham feeling tired and weak.

When Monday morning arrived, Greig awoke to find his son sitting up in bed watching TV, some of the color back in his cheeks. While he looked better, the dark circles around his eyes told just how rough the past thirty-six hours had been.

Sitting up, Greig wiped the sleep away from his eyes and tried to keep his swollen bladder in check for a few more minutes. "You look better, kiddo. How are you feeling?" Greig asked, surprised at how gravelly his voice sounded.

"Better than yesterday, but still sore and tired."

"Do you feel well enough to hit the road today? It's about a four-hour drive to Nana and Grankie's."

"You bet."

"Good. Why don't you take a shower, and I'll start packing up our things. I need to send a couple of emails to Timothy and work, and then we can be on the road."

Graham flipped open the lid of his suitcase and pulled out a clean set of clothes, not bothering to check to see if anything matched. He closed the door to the bathroom, the sound of running water beginning a few moments later.

Pulling out his laptop and plug adapter, Greig fired up Windows, logged onto the hotel WiFi, and logged into his email account. Despite being out of office, he expected to see a ton of unread messages, but there were only a few, none of which were important. He hammered out a short message to Timothy, letting him know where they were headed next and asking if everything was going well at the office.

Punctual and efficient as always, Tim responded in a matter of minutes, assuring his boss that all was well and informing him of a new project that he had landed over the weekend. Greig couldn't help but be happy, recognizing just how similar Timothy was to the younger version of himself. He hadn't given much thought to what he would do after the trip was over and things progressed with Graham, but he suddenly felt as though his time with the company was coming to an end.

Just as old man Charles had suggested, Greig has spent more and more time working from home, more out of necessity than a desire to be out of the office. It had been difficult initially, but he had a crack team on board, so he seldom had little to do other than designate work and approve new hires. His house was paid off, and he had more money in the bank than he could ever spend, so why continue to work.

He and Lisa had traveled a lot when they first met, and while he and Graham had gone to a few places over the years, his desire to hit the open road had vanished. In the matter of a couple of days, his wanderlust had returned, and he was ready to visit countries he had always dreamed of going to but had never made the time to visit. Mind made up, Greig decided that he would call his lawyer as soon as possible and put the business's long-term running in Timothy Allen's hands. Greig closed the lid of the laptop, rubbed his hands together, and set about packing their gear. For the first time in years, he felt truly happy, but as Graham stepped out of the bathroom, a towel wrapped around his waist, Greig noticed how visible the boy's ribs were and how frail he looked. The happiness he had felt just moments before was pulled down to his gut by the weight of the rock that was Graham's impending death.

Forcing a smile, he said, "Everything okay?"

"I forgot my brush." Fiddling around in his suitcase, Graham let out a yelp of victory as he found the hairbrush beneath a pile of clothes. He ran it through his wet hair as he vanished into the steam billowing out of the bathroom door.

Greig exhaled loudly and got back to work, mentally preparing himself for the drive ahead of him.

***

The first part of the journey had passed without a hitch, but as they headed further north, the multiple lane motorways gave way to narrower country roads where approaching vehicles looked to be on a collision course.

Greig gripped the steering wheel tightly, a dull ache spreading across his forehead and stretching like an elastic band all the way around to the back of his head. Graham had been asleep for the past hour, which was a bit of a blessing given that he hadn't stopped talking for the first couple of hours.

When the road started hugging the coastline and the Atlantic Ocean came into view, Greig decided to nudge his son awake, so he could see. It took a moment for him to blink away the last of the fog from his sleep, but once it was gone, the boy found it impossible to peel his eyes away from the view outside his window.

"The ocean is so big. It looks like it stretches forever."

"Wait till I show you Corbies Peak in Kilbrennan. The view from up there is unbelievable."

"What's that big island out there?"

"That's the Isle of Skye, and beyond that is the Hebrides. We can catch a ferry to both of them during our trip if you fancy it."

"A boat trip would be super cool."

"Want to hear something even cooler?"

"What's that?"

"We can take the car on the ferry."

"No way."

"Did I lie to you about the castle in the middle of the street?"

Graham looked around the inside of the car and then out at the ocean. He gave a little shrug and went back to asking questions about the villages they passed through, most of which Greig could answer.

Before long, they began to climb a gradual incline that seemed endless. Once the road eventually leveled out, a sign saying "Welcome to Kilbrennan" flashed past on the side of the road.

"We're here," Graham yelled.

"Almost." Greig drove for about a mile more, but just before they began the downhill drive into the village that was now visible in the distance, he pulled into a parking lot sitting at the edge of a large green space. "Let's go for a quick walk."

They left the car behind and walked along a paved pathway that skirted around a soccer field. Graham stopped for a moment, watching the boys play, their happy voices carrying across the park on the wind that blew in off the ocean.

"That's where me and my pals used to play football when we were kids. I think we spent most of our childhood up here, kicking a ball around or throwing stones off Corbies Peak."

"Where is that?" Grahan asked, still keeping one eye on the game.

They rounded a bend and came upon a pair of benches looking out over the water. "Here we are," Greig said, sitting on the bench and patting the space beside him." Graham took a seat and stared out at the vast expanse of the ocean.

Beyond the pathway was a stretch of grass about two feet wide, followed by a sheer drop down to the water.

"How high up are we?" Graham asked.

"Probably about a hundred feet or so. I honestly don't know. There's a beach at the foot of the cliff, but you can only go at certain times of the day."

"Why's that."

"Well, when the tide comes in, it completely covers the beach. On stormy days, you can sit up here and feel the spray coming off the waves as they smash into the cliff."

Graham turned and looked back at the soccer field, and then once again out at the ocean. "Did you ever lose a ball over the edge?"

"All the time. There's a little shop in town that serves just about everything you can imagine. I would guess, though, that a large chunk of the profits came from selling soccer balls, as we had to buy a new one every couple of weeks."

Lifting himself up on the bench, Graham tried his best to peer over the edge, but fear got the better of him. He gave an involuntary shudder as he sat back down. "Has anyone, you know, ever fallen off?"

"No, although they did toy with the idea of putting up fences after a kid jumped on a dare."

Graham's eyes went wide.

"He waited until high tide and then took a running jump off the edge, all so he could claim the prize of a pile of candy that a bunch of other kids ponied up as the prize."

"Did he…"

"He was fine, save for a broken ankle. He got fortunate."

"Did you know him, Dad?"

Greig leaned over and whispered in his son's ear. "Let's just say I was one of the kids that put candy in the prize pile. Malcolm was my best friend, and I'm positive you'll meet him today."

"Whoa! Can I ask him about the jump when I meet him?"

"He would love nothing more. I think he's told the story a million times, and it gets better with every retelling. It's chilly up here. How about we go see Nana and Grankie now?"

"Yeah. It's going to be so cool to see them in person finally. I don't remember the last time we were here."

"You were just a wee boy then. I barely remember much about it."

They sat for a few more minutes, staring out at the ocean, then they made their way back to the car and headed down into the village.

Chapter Ten

Rather than taking the street that led to his parents' house, Greig drove on into the village center and onto what passed as their main street. He told himself that he was doing it to show off more of his childhood home to Graham, but the fact of the matter was that he was playing a game of avoidance.

Greig loved his Mum and Dad, but he also harbored some resentment towards them. He had asked them to come to the States, on his dime, when Lisa died, but they had made all kinds of excuses for not being able to leave. Greig had asked again several times after that and been met with the same litany of feeble excuses. He eventually stopped asking, but the frustration and anger remained.

It had been more than ten years since his last visit, but the old place looked the same. Fishing boats bobbed in the harbor while fishermen sat on the stone dock, mending nets and telling tall tales.

The row of shops along the waterfront was still the same, as was the pub, The Golden Pheasant, which sat at the end of the street. Greig toyed with the idea of going in to see who was there, but he knew that his mum would get in the huff if she found out that he had stopped for a pint before heading home.

He pulled into the pub's parking lot, turned the car around, and headed towards his parents' place. No more than two minutes later, he turned onto their street and parked in front of the brick house that also had changed little since he was last there. It looked as though some repairs had been made to the roof, as a few of the tiles were a brighter shade of orange than the others. The curtains, which had a wildflower pattern, were different, and the garden path was repaved, but other than that, it was the house he remembered.

He saw the curtains move quickly, and then the front door flew open as his mum came tearing out of the house, drying her hands on a dishtowel as she tried her best to run in her fur-lined house slippers. His dad held back, leaning against the doorframe, a pipe hanging out of his mouth.

Lorna practically dragged Graham out of the car, pulling him into a hug that threatened to smother him. She rocked back and forth, planting kisses on his head and telling him how handsome he was through wracking sobs. When she finally let him go and made her way to Grieg, his face was flushed, and he was grinning from ear to ear.

The welcome for Greig was less enthusiastic but still warm. "He looks so thin," Lorna whispered. "Is he eating?"

Grieg glanced over her shoulder and watched as his son and his father high-fived and went on for a hug. "Off and on. Some days he eats like a regular teenager; others, it's a struggle to get anything into him."

"We'll make sure he's well looked after. Come away in. I'll pop the kettle on."

Stepping inside the house, Greig felt as though he had stepped back in time. The only real difference was that a gas heater had replaced the old coal fireplace. He was also amazed that the house seemed so small and cramped. It had seemed cavernous when he was young, but the two-bedroom building was probably a third of the size of his home in Atlanta.

Lorna headed off to the kitchen to make a pot of tea while Greig went through to the living room. His dad sat in a battered chair beside the heater that sat in front of the bricked-up fireplace, relighting his pipe while listening to Graham tell stories about their trip so far.

"Hold on a wee minute, son. I want to hear all about your adventures, but let me say hello to your daddy." Gary hauled himself out of the chair, which seemed perfectly molded to his body, and reached out to shake his son's hand. He looked for a moment as though he was going to pull Greig in for an embrace, but the moment passed. "Good to see you in the flesh again, my boy."

"Yes, you too, Dad."

Greig moved over to the couch and sat down. Leaning back, he stretched his legs out and went to place his feet on the coffee table just as his mother walked in with a large teapot and cups on a silver tray.

"Don't you dare put your stinky feet on my table," she yelled.

"My socks are clean, Mum."

"Nonsense." She placed the tray on the table and then flicked her tea towel at Greig's legs. "Right, who wants a cuppa?" Without waiting for a response, she poured for everyone and handed out the cups, leaning down to kiss Graham every time she passed him.

Greig winced as he took a sip of the tea, which was scalding, and burned his tongue. "So, Mum, do they still do the steak pies down at The Golden Pheasant?"

Lorna folded her arms across her chest and kicked out at her husband. "Are you hearing this,

Gary? Your boy wants to know if they still do the steak pies at the pub."

"Of course I bloody hear him, woman. I'm sitting two feet away. Aye, son, they still do the pies, and aye, your old mum is still their lone supplier."

"Brilliant. I thought we might head down later for a bite to eat. I want to meet up with Malcolm and the rest of the lads, introduce them to Graham."

Sniffing loudly, Lorna fished out her tissue and began dabbing at her eyes.

"What's wrong, Mum," Greig asked.

"It's your first night back home. I thought you might want to spend some time with your dad and me before swanning off with your pals."

"I said that we should go, which means you and dad, too."

"I could have made a big steak pie for dinner if I'd known what time you were getting in, but I suppose I could go for a wee gin and tonic and take a night off from being your dad's servant."

Gary rolled his eyes as he took a big draw on his pipe, blowing out smoke that was sweet and woody smelling. "That sounds like a cracking idea, son. I could murder a pint. We could walk down. It's a nice enough day."

"That might be a good idea if we are all planning on having a drink," Greig said. "You up for a walk, Graham?"

"Will the pub have Irn-Bru there?"

"They will, not to mention all kinds of crisps and nuts," Gary said between puffs.

"Crisps?"

"Chips, and by nuts, I think Grankie might be talking about the people that drink there. Is crazy Davie still on the go?"

"Aye, and still full of shite."

"Mind your language in front of the boy," Lorna scolded.

"I'm sure he's heard much worse, dear. Kids nowadays have mouths like sailors."

"A lot of my friends say shit, Nana, but I don't."

The adults all tried to avoid eye contact, but it didn't matter. Gary broke first, letting out a roar of a laugh that proved to be infectious. Graham looked at his dad and his grandparents, bemused at why they were laughing. "What did I say?"

"You didn't say shit, son," Gary said, setting off a fresh round of laughter.

***

The walk to the pub was a short one, but they took their time to get there, enjoying the conversation and each other's company. When they were within a hundred yards of the bar, Graham jogged ahead to act as the doorman for his family. Gary was the last one in, and he reached into his pocket and pulled out a coin, which he slipped into Graham's hand. "Wonderful service, son," he said.

Stepping into the pub was like going from night into day. Dark wooden paneling covered every wall, and heavy wooden beams served as roof supports. The lights were dimmed to the point of almost being off, with the primary source of illumination coming from a fruit machine and a jukebox tucked away in the corner.

Save for a young couple, and a man slumped over a pint at the bar, the place was empty, so finding a table was not an issue. "I'll get the first round in," Gary said. "Do you want to give your old grankie a hand with the drinks, Graham?"

Graham nodded excitedly but then looked at his dad to make sure it was okay.

"I'll have a pint of Tennent's, wee man."

"How's business, Colin?" Gary asked as he strolled up to the bar.

The bartender was a brute of a man, all hair and tattoos, his bushy beard covering most of his face. To Graham, he looked like Hagrid from the Harry Potter movies. "Just waiting on the rush, Gary. They'll all be in once they get cleaned up after a day out fishing. Is that your boy over there?"

"It is, and this is my grandson, Graham."

"Nice to meet you, young man. What are you after? A pint or a whiskey?"

Graham looked over to his dad sitting on the opposite side of the pub and said, "My dad's here. Better just make it an Irn-Bru."

The comment set Colin laughing, his face turning the color of beetroot as he struggled to catch his breath. "Irn-Bru it is. I'll even throw in a free bag of crisps for the entertainment."

"We'll have two Tennent's and a G and T, too, please," Gary said as he pulled out his wallet.

"Put that away," Colin said as he poured the first pint. "This round is on me. Tell your lad I said hello."

"Cheers, Colin, I will." Gary reached over and gave the man a nudge at the bar, which made him sit up straight and grab his pint. "How are you doing, Davie?"

Winking and making a clicking sound with his mouth, he replied, "Top shelf, thanks for asking."

Placing all the drinks on a tray, Colin handed it over to Gary. He then reached under the bar and came up with three different flavors of crisps, which he gave to Graham. "I'm not sure what you like, so you might as well have one of each."

"Thank you, mister Colin."

"Just Colin is fine, or you can call me Hagrid like all the other kids do."

Graham almost dropped his chips, thinking that giant of a man had read his mind.

"Can you put us on four steak pies, too?"

"Not a problem."

Back at the table, they sipped their drinks and slipped into comfortable conversation, talking about life in the village compared to life in the big city. They ate and complimented Lorna on her steak pies while the pub began to fill.

The quiet pub grew steadily louder as the patrons talked and laughed after a hard day's work. The jukebox sprang to life, playing songs from the eighties, and the fruit machines coughed out coins for a lucky winner.

Greig was at the bar ordering the next round of drinks when the front door burst open, and a voice called out, "Well, well, well, the prodigal son has returned."

Spinning around, Greig came face to face with his childhood friend Malcolm. Save for a bit of a belly, he looked the same as he did when they were kids. He had the same buzz cut and that crooked grin that always made him look as though he was up to no good, which he very often was. "Bloody hell, Malcolm, how have you not aged?" Greig said, pulling his friend in for a hug.

"I know, I'm an Adonis. I wasn't sure it was you at first. The glare off your bald spot blinded me. What happened there?"

Greig tapped his friend on the belly and said, "Looks like you might have eaten it." They both laughed and hugged again. "Grab your drink and come over and sit with us."

Malcolm looked over to the corner and waved over to Lorna and Gary. "Is that your wee lad?" he asked.

"It is."

"Handsome wee bugger." The sparkle went out of Malcolm's eyes for a moment as he placed a hand on Greig's shoulder. "How are you both holding up?"

"As best we can."

"If you need anything while you're here, don't be too proud to ask?"

"I will, mate. By the way, any luck with the tickets?"

Malcolm puffed out his cheeks and exhaled slowly. "It's a nightmare. No luck yet, but I still have a few weeks. I'll keep trying."

They clinked glasses and took a drink from their pints as an Elton John song came on the jukebox.

"Elton fucking John," Davie slurred loudly.

"What's that, Davie?" Malcolm asked, winking at Greig.

"It was back during my time doing gigs in London. I played this little club, singing some of the old standards. Little did I know, Elton fucking John was in the audience. He bought me a drink after the show and told me that mine was the best voice he'd ever heard."

"I didn't know you were a singer."

"I was a top biller at all the top clubs. Elton wanted to take me on tour as an opener, but the dirty bastard tried to grab my arse, and that was the end of it. I'm a professional, not a toyboy."

113

"So close, and yet so far, Davie," Malcolm said.

They made their way through the crowd, but Malcolm reached out and grabbed Grieg's arm before they got to the table. "I know you're not a fan of surprises, pal, so I should warn you that your old girlfriend is coming in tonight."

"What? Geraldine Rogers, I thought she lived in Glasgow with her fiancé."

"She did up until a few months ago. She moved back to take care of her parents' house after her mum died and hasn't left since."

Greig's heart began to pound. He hadn't seen his ex since moving to Atlanta all those years ago, and he worried that she might still be mad at him for ditching her. The more he thought about, though, the more foolish that notion seemed. Many years had passed since then, so surely she wouldn't harbor any ill feelings. He sat at the table and watched as Malcolm spun his broken ankle yarn to Graham, the boy staring at him in wide-eyed wonder. He hadn't been back more than a few hours, but Kilbrennan was beginning to feel like home again.

.

Chapter Eleven

Given that it was a Monday night, the bar had mostly cleared out when the door swung open, and Geradine Rogers stepped inside. Malcolm saw her first, so he hissed at Greig to get his attention and nodded his head in her direction.

She wore jeans, a faded University of Glasgow sweatshirt, and a pair of Converse sneakers. She didn't have any makeup on, but she didn't need it. Her pale skin and slender cheekbones, all perfectly framed by her red hair, styled in a pixie cut.

"The usual, Geraldine?" Colin called out from behind the bar.

"Yes, please." She moved towards the bar, taking a moment to scan the pub. When her gaze fell upon the corner table, she stopped in mid-stride and said, "Oh, my god. Is that you, Greig Ramsay?"

"Guilty as charged," he said meekly.

She raised a finger, moved to the bar to grab her drink, and then made her way over to the table. "Hello, Mr. and Mrs. Ramsay, lovely to see you. Hey, Malcolm." She turned her attention to Graham, her green eyes twinkling as she smiled at him. "And who might you be?"

"I'm Graham. Greig is my dad,"

"I thought that might be it. You look just like him. Do you mind if I sit beside you?"

Graham shook his head and moved over, making space for her.

"When did you get into town?" she asked Greig.

"Earlier today. We had a couple of days in Glasgow and Edinburgh before driving up."

Turning to Graham, Geraldine asked, "Did you visit the castle."

"We did."

"What was your favorite part?"

"When they fired off the gun at one o'clock. I thought they were attacking the city."

117

Geraldine laughed and leaned in closer. "Between you and me, I thought the same thing the first time I saw it."

Malcolm stood to order another round of drinks, but Lorna waved him off. "Nothing for me, dear, I'll never make it home at this rate."

"What about the rest of you?" Malcolm asked.

"I'll take another," Geraldine said.

Gary fell in line with his wife, although he looked none too happy about it. Greig turned to Graham and asked. "What about you, wee man?"

"I'm full, dad, but I was wondering if you could show me how to play that machine over there, the one where you can win money."

"I'm not sure if you're allowed."

"Hold on," Malcolm said. "Colin, do you mind if the wee man has a shot on the fruit machine?"

"Of course not. Have at it."

Greig led his son over to the machine and lifted him onto a barstool to make it easier to reach the buttons. He fed some money into the dispenser, and the machine lit up, playing a happy tune and flashing lights all over. "Right. It's easy enough. All you need to do is hit the big orange button that says spin."

They watched as the reels spun, the fruits and bells not lining up in a winning combination. After a few spins, Graham said, "Geraldine is really nice."

"She is that."

"Was she your girlfriend when you lived here?"

"Why would you ask that?" Greig asked, trying to hide his embarrassment.

"It looks as though you like each other, and she sure is pretty."

"Wait a minute. I thought you said girls my age were gross."

Graham gave his father the side-eye, a cheeky grin on his face, and said, "Maybe I like redheads. If you want to stay for a little bit longer with your friends, I can walk home with Nana and Grankie."

Looking over at the table, Greig caught the group laughing and having a good time. He wanted to stay longer, but he also didn't want to ditch his son on their first day back. He felt torn and didn't know what to say. "I'll see them again while we are here."

"How about this," Graham said, "if we win on the next spin, you stay. If we lose, then we go home." He held out his hand for a fist bump, to which Greig obliged.

The wheels spun one more time and showed nothing but bells. The music blared, and money started dropping into the collection tray at the bottom of the machine. The people still in the bar hollered and broke into a spontaneous round of applause.

Greig tousled his son's hair. "I guess I'm staying."

***

As soon as his dad called to let them know they had made it home safely, Greig began to relax. He relaxed further when Malcolm called it a night, promising to take another run at getting tickets to the game in the morning.

They sat quietly for a moment before Geraldine broke the silence. "Imagine my surprise coming in here and seeing you tonight."

"Yeah, it caught me off guard, too. I was scared you might be mad at me still."

"No. I was when you left, but I also understood your reason for going. How has life treated you in America."

Greig sighed and launched into the story of his life since leaving Kilbrennan. He wasn't sure why he felt so comfortable telling it all to

Geraldine, but by the time he finished, she had reached across the table and taken his hands, tears streaming down her cheeks.

"And there's nothing they can do for your boy?"

Greig shook his head.

"That breaks my heart. He seems like a brilliant little laddie."

"He is. He's the best." Greig rubbed her hand and looked into her eyes. "Listen, I really am sorry for leaving the way I did. I know it hurt my mum and dad, too. It was selfish of me."

"Most of us leave here eventually but isn't it funny how we all find our way back? We're like salmon, swimming upstream to return to the place where we were born."

"Are you planning on staying?"

"I don't know yet. What about you?"

Greig shrugged. I've been trying to think beyond Graham, but it's tough to focus on anything else. There is something special about this wee village, though. I think it's the people and how very little changes. Progress is not all it's cracked up to be."

They both jumped when a bell rang behind the bar. "Last orders, everyone," Colin yelled.

"I think I've had enough," Geraldine said. "A bit of fresh air on the way home might help."

"Malcolm says you're living in your parents' house, is that right?"

"Yes, I am."

"Then please allow me to walk you home. It's on the way."

"I'd like that," Geraldine smiled.

They shared childhood stories as they walked, the breeze blowing in off the harbor cold but not freezing. Greig would have liked it to last longer, but it was only a few minutes before they were at Geraldine's doorstep.

"I had a great night, Greig. It was nice to see you again."

"You, too. Maybe we can get together again. I'm sure Graham would love it. He confided in me tonight that he has a thing for redheads."

"Smart boy, just like his daddy. I'd love that." She leaned over and gave Greig a peck on the cheek, her lips brushing against his as she pulled away. "Goodnight. Give Graham a hug for me."

The exterior light was on at his parents' house when he got back, the front door left unlocked. He stepped in quietly, locking it behind him. Kicking off his shoes, he peeked into the living room and saw that the couch was made up and ready for him to sleep on. He tip-toed upstairs and sat on the edge of Graham's bed.

"How was your date, Dad?"

"It wasn't a date, you nosy bugger."

"I hope we get to hang out with her again. You should ask her. I bet Mom wouldn't mind."

"I don't think she would either, which is why I already asked."

"Good," Graham mumbled before falling asleep.

Greig lay on the couch and stared at the ceiling, finding it impossible to nod off. He thought of Geraldine and how good she looked and how comfortable it was to talk to her. Part of the reason he hadn't found anyone else after Lisa was because that level of comfort was always missing. When sleep did finally come, it was Geraldine that was the last thing he thought about.

Chapter Twelve

The next ten days were a blur, with a host of day trips packed into the schedule. Geraldine was along for most of them, and Graham, for the most part, held up like a champ. It all went south on day eleven, when the craziness of their travels finally seemed to catch up.

Greig sat beside the bed and watched his son sleep, his breaths coming in fits and starts as he seemed to struggle to take in air. The boy had consumed nothing but fluids for the past couple of days and now looked gaunt and frail. Greig cursed himself for pushing so hard and not giving his son a break, but he has been healthy and happy the entire time.

The bedroom door opened slowly, and Lorna came in carrying a tray. "Is he still sleeping? I made him some chicken broth," she whispered.

"Yes, Mum, he's still out for the count."

Lorna set the tray on the bedside table and then pulled up a chair beside her son. She sat down with a sigh and rested her hands on the bed. "What about you, son? Are you hungry? I can make you a sandwich or something."

"Thanks, Mum, but I don't think I could eat."

She nodded and went to stand, but Greig took her hand and gently kept her in place.

"Can I ask you something?" he said.

"Of course you can."

"Why did you and Dad never come to visit? I asked so many times?"

Lorna fiddled with her apron and took a moment to answer. "Your dad and I are set in our ways, always have been. Neither one of us have ever gone far beyond this town. If you remember, any time you went anywhere outside of Kilbrennan, it was always your dad who took you."

"I understand that, Mum, but what about after Lisa died?"

127

"That broke our hearts, but we knew you had a good support system. Your boss was a wonderful man, and you had great friends."

Greig's head drooped as though it was too heavy for his neck to bear. "That's all true, but sometimes a boy just needs his mum. I needed you…I needed you." He put his head in his hands as the dam broke and the tears fell.

Pulling him close, Lorna hugged her son and cried along with him. "I'm so sorry. You were always so bloody independent, but a mother should know when her child is in need."

They say together for what seemed like an eternity, Lorna trying to replace her guilt with the grief that poured out of her son. She wished she could take all his pain and all his fear and make it go away for him. She also wanted to swap places with Graham and take his sickness, but since both were impossible, Lorna simply held Greig until he cried himself out.

"Thank you," Greig finally mumbled.

"You know you can stay here as long as you want. There's no need to go back anytime soon."

"I know, Mum."

Lorna put her hand under his chin and raised his head. "Your dad and I are so proud of you. Look at what you've done with your life." She turned and nodded toward Graham. "Look at the wonderful wee man you have raised. I'll bet Lisa is looking down on you and smiling."

"I hope so."

"I'm going to call our doctor and have him come take a look, maybe see if there is something he can do."

"He does house calls?"

"Under the right circumstances, and I think it's fair to say that this fits the bill," Lorna said.

***

Greig, Lorna, and Gary watched as Dr. McDonald examined Graham, who slipped in and out of sleep throughout it all. "Well, given his Hodgkin's diagnosis, he is right about where we would expect him to be. I hate to say it, but it's probably going to be a relatively quick decline from this point forward."

Lorna sobbed loudly and ran out of the bedroom, while Gary stuck his pipe in his mouth to prevent himself from crying.

"What can we do for him?" Greig asked.

"Keep him as comfortable as possible and get some fluids into him. He's a little dehydrated right now. Gatorade or Lucozade will help, so if you need to wake him up to get fluids in, don't be afraid to do it."

"I'll run to the shop and get some now," Gary said, leaving his son and the doctor alone in the room with Graham.

"How much longer does he have?"

"A week or two would be my guess, but it is just a guess. It's almost impossible to know for sure."

Greig nodded. "Thank you for coming out. I appreciate it."

As they shook hands, the doctor said, "I know you'll want to sit by his bed from now until the end, but take some time for yourself, especially over the next few days when you still have time to get away for a minute. It's okay to do that."

"I don't know…"

"Listen to me, son. Your mum and dad are here to help. Getting down the pub for an hour while he's asleep is not a cardinal sin. If you need anything else from me, I'm only a phone call away."

They shook hands again, and the doctor left, stopping in at the kitchen to check on Lorna before he headed out. Greig took up his usual spot beside the bed and watched his son sleep. When his dad returned with the beverages, he managed to get Graham awake for a moment and get some fluids into him before the boy drifted off again.

Pulling out his phone, Greig saw that he had missed a pair of text messages, one each from Malcolm and Geraldine. They both wanted to meet him at The Golden Pheasant later in the day. He went to pocket the phone without responding, but taking a moment to think about what the doctor had said, he messaged them back and agreed to meet up.

***

Malcolm and Geraldine were both already in the pub and sitting at the bar when Greig arrived. Crazy Davie had his head on the bar and looked to be asleep, although he still had a half-full pint of lager in a death grip.

Greig took the stool beside Geraldine and nodded a thank you to Colin when the barman placed a cooled beer in front of him. Rather than waiting for them to ask, he quickly filled them in on the latest with Graham, the news greeted with hugs and mumbled apologies.

"I'm sorry I can't hang around," Malcolm said. "I wanted to tell you in person that I couldn't get the tickets for the game. I do, though, have an alternate plan."

"Not a problem, pal; I knew it was a tough ask. What's the other plan?"

"Instead of getting Graham to the game, we bring it to him."

Geraldine screwed up her face and looked at Malcolm. "What does that mean?"

"I've been talking to some of the lads at The Red Lion pub in Craigmoor, and they are all about coming here as the visiting team in a game against the local lads up at the park. They'll wear white shirts and be England, while we wear blue and play as Scotland. We'll be playing for the Graham Ramsay Cup, which Colin here will kindly donate."

The bartop groaned as Colin leaned on it, tears brimming in his eyes. "We'll play the game on Saturday, and then I'll open up on Sunday so we can all come here and watch the actual game together. I'll put on some food and maybe buy a round or two."

Davie raised his head off the bar and said, "I can get Hector McMillan to come and coach us."

"Hector McMillan? Scotland manager Hector McMillan? I think he might be a wee bit busy this weekend," Malcolm said, rolling his eyes and shaking his head.

"He's a good lad. We played together when I was selected for the regional team in high school. I was the better player, but he had a good tactical head on him. I knew he'd make a good manager."

"Is that right, Davie? Was this before your singing career?"

"I mean, obviously before. I was too young to sing in the clubs. I went into acting after I did my knee in, and I had a wee fling with Meryl Streep. Poor lassie couldn't understand a word I said. We were doomed to failure. It was then…" In mid-sentence, Davie blinked heavily and rested his head back on the bar.

"Silly old bastard," Malcolm mumbled. "So, what do you think?"

"I think it's a brilliant idea, but I'm not sure what kind of shape Graham is going to be in this weekend."

Geraldine placed a hand on Greig's arm. "We'll get him there. My mum's old wheelchair is still at the house. We can get him around in that and make sure that he is warm during the game."

"Right then. I'll let him know. He'll be excited, I bet."

Malcolm downed his pint and rushed off to take care of all the last-minute details. Geraldine and Greig moved to the table beside the jukebox when Davie's snoring became too much to bear.

"That's an amazing thing that Malcolm and Colin are doing," Greig said, taking a sip of his drink.

"They are lovely people. They stepped up to help when I moved back."

135

"You're not so bad yourself," Greig said, blushing furiously. "These past couple of weeks have been superb, and you've been a big part of that."

"It has been my pleasure. I haven't had this much fun in forever. I only wish it were in different circumstances."

"Same."

Geraldine picked at the corner of her beer coaster, picking away the top layer in little pieces. "Have you given any thought to what you are going to do? Are you staying or going back home?"

"My mum asked me to stay. I think I might do that for a bit. It's grim to talk about it, but Graham has always seemed Scottish at heart. I want to scatter his ashes here so that he is always a small part of this place."

"That's lovely, Greig."

"What about you? What are your plans?"

"I don't know. My fiancé has asked me to move back to Glasgow."

"Ah, I see," Greig said, taking another drink.

"The thing is, I believe my heart belongs here. I think I might be…"

The jukebox kicked on and picked a song at random, as it always did when it had been sitting idle for a while. Greig felt his blood run cold as the opening bars of *You're the Best Thing* began to play. Reaching back, he forcefully yanked the plug out of the wall, instantly silencing the jukebox.

"You don't like The Style Council?" Geraldine asked with a smile.

"Yes, no, well, it's complicated. That was our song," he mumbled.

"You and your wife?"

"Yes. Sorry, that was rude. What were you saying?"

Geraldine pushed her empty glass aside and cleared her throat. "Erm, nothing really. Just that I haven't decided what I'm going to do yet."

The conversation turned awkward after that and ended when Geraldine announced that she needed to get home. "I'll stop in and see you both tomorrow."

"Let me pay up, and I'll walk you home," Greig said.

"That's okay. I need to run a couple of errands, but I'll see you tomorrow."

Watching her go, Greig balled his fist and slammed it into the side of the jukebox, drawing a concerned stare from Colin. Slipping on his jacket, he went to the bar and paid for his and Davie's tab. "Thanks again, Colin, for everything."

"Not a problem, mate. We'll make it a weekend to remember for your boy.

Walking slowly up the street and feeling a little sorry for himself, Greig peeked inside each of the shop windows, hoping to catch a glimpse of Geraldine, but all he saw was his own miserable reflection staring back.

Back at the house, he went into the living room, where his dad was sitting reading the paper. "Where's Mum?" he asked.

"Upstairs with Graham. We've been taking it in shifts to make sure he's never alone when he wakes up."

"Thanks, Dad. Can you do me a favor?"

"What is it?" Gary asked, folding up the paper and shoving it down at his side.

"Can you stand up for a minute?"

The old man looked confused, but he set his pipe aside and stood up, wincing a little as Greig moved towards him and pulled him into a hug. After a moment, his body relaxed, and he put his arms around his son. "I love you, lad. You and your boy and your mum are my world. I should have told you that more often."

Greig said nothing. He just continued to hold on tight, the smell of tobacco on his father's close conjuring up childhood memories of nights sitting by the fire listening to his old man tell stories behind a veil of pipe smoke. "You told me now. That's all that matters," he said as he pulled away from the embrace. "Come on upstairs. I have some news to share."

When they got to the bedroom, Graham was awake and drinking a large glass of Lucozade while Laura tried to talk him into taking some soup. The boy's eyes lit up when his dad walked in the room, but they positively glowed when Greig shared the news of the weekend plans.

"I'm sorry we won't get to go to the actual game," Greig said.

"That's okay, Dad. It'll be fun to watch with all our friends. Plus, I'll get to see my dad play for Scotland. You are playing, right?"

Greig thought about it for a moment. "I suppose I am."

Chapter Thirteen

Greig wasn't a man who believed in miracles, but he had to admit that they had gotten more than a little lucky. The Saturday weather was perfect, the sun shining, and the North Atlantic's waters as smooth as a pane of glass. It looked as though the entire village was present, not to mention several visitors that had traveled in with the Cragmoor lads.

The best part of all, though, was that Graham was full of life. He still looked frail, but his spirits were high, and they lifted further when Malcolm and the other locals from the pub presented him with the new Scotland jersey, which he slipped over his sweatshirt with a little help from Geraldine, who was acting as his wheelchair pilot.

As they approached the park, the crowd broke into a rousing chorus of cheers and applause. Colin, who had a microphone attached to a small amp, announced Graham's arrival and directed him

141

to a roped-off area beside a table where a tall silver trophy sat. Geraldine wheeled Graham into the VIP area, where Lorna and Gary were already seated, and sat beside him as Colin announced the teams.

"Ladies and gentlemen, will you please give a warm welcome to our English visitors today."

A group of players on the opposite side of the field, all dressed in white, stepped onto the field and waved. The crowd booed loudly, with the visitors from Craigmoor joining in. The men may have been their friends and family, but all bets were off when they were representing England.

"And now, let's hear it for Scotland, and let's give an extra special cheer to team captain Greig Ramsay."

Cheers and whistles rang across the park and soon turned into a chant of "Scotland, Scotland, Scotland." The opposing teams' players lined up in the middle of the park and shook hands before posing for pictures, after which the referee for the day blew his whistle to let them all know that the game was about to start.

"How exciting is this?" Geraldine asked Graham, who was applauding and cheering for his dad.

"It hasn't even started, and it's already better than any game I've ever seen on television."

The whistle blew, and the game began. What the players lacked in skill, they made up for in passion, chasing down every pass and crunching into every tackle. It was a frantic opening ten minutes, but it was a pace that the pub regulars, many of whom were getting up there in years, could never hope to maintain.

The game settled into a more leisurely pace, and it was England who struck first. A long hopeful shot somehow squirmed through the hands of the goalkeeper and into the back of the net, eliciting another round of boos from the crowd.

With half-time approaching, the pace had slowed to a crawl, but Malcolm still seemed to have some energy. He latched onto a bad pass and went through on goal, sliding the ball home to even up the score. The fans lining the pitch roared in delight, blotting out the sound of the half-time whistle, while Graham and Geraldine almost toppled the wheelchair as they hugged.

Colin went around the local lads handing out whiskey shots as they tried to catch their breath during the break. "That'll put some fire in your bellies," he roared. "Get them down you." They threw back the drinks and watched as a figure came walking towards them from the far end of the park.

"Is that crazy Davie?" someone asked.

"Can't be. He's walking upright and in a straight line," Malcolm said.

As he got closer, another of the locals said, "Fuck me, it is him."

Davie strode across the field dressed in a tracksuit and a battered pair of football boots. He was clean-shaven, and his grey hair glistened in the sun courtesy of some shiny product that was holding everything in place. "Who's in charge here," he demanded as he approached the sideline.

Everyone pointed at Malcolm, not wanting to deal with what was coming. "Bastards," Malcolm hissed out the side of his mouth. "What can I do for you, Davie?"

"Why was I not invited to be part of this team?"

"No offense, pal, but you are in your sixties and seldom sober."

"That's as may be, but I'm sober today and ready to go in. What's the score?"

"All tied up at one," Greig said.

"Right. Hold them off as best you can, and then throw me in for the last five minutes."

Before the conversation could go any further, the referee blew the whistle and signaled the players back to the field.

The second-half began as the first ended, with everyone struggling to keep up the pace. Greig put Scotland in front and found the energy to sprint over to his son, where he slid on his knees to celebrate the goal. Graham was hopping up and down in delight, which Lorna put an end to quickly, easing him back into his wheelchair and placing a blanket over his legs.

The game restarted, and within a matter of minutes, it was tied again. With both sets of players now looking exhausted, it was only a matter of time before someone went down. Kenny Taylor, the local butcher, was that man. He went over on his ankle trying to chase down an errant pass, and when he tried to get up, his ankle refused to co-operate. "I'm done, lads," he said.

"Can you not hobble about for the last couple of minutes?" Malcolm asked.

"Hobble about? I can barely bloody stand." They helped him off the field, where Colin was there to meet him with another shot.

Malcolm looked over towards Davie, who was standing on the sideline, gripping the sides of his pants. "Alright, you crazy old bastard, on you come."

After a couple of quick stretches, Davie ripped off his tearaway pants, receiving a few wolf whistles from the ladies in the crowd, and tossed them aside. The tracksuit top was next to go, but he jogged over to Graham with that garment and handed him the jacket. "A wee souvenir for you, son."

"That man is out of his bloody mind," Gary said, trying to stifle a laugh.

Davie jogged to the middle of the field and shouted at the other players on his team, "Get it to me when you have a chance."

The play continued, with England applying some pressure. They came close to scoring, but one of the local boys thumped the ball upfield. It seemed to hang in the air for an eternity before dropping in the direction of Davie, who controlled the ball perfectly on his chest. He let it fall to his feet and turned upfield, noticing Greig making a run down the right-hand side. He placed an inch-perfect pass to Greig's feet and started heading towards the goal.

Greig took the ball in stride and found the energy to get past an England defender. He looked up and spotted Davie arriving at the edge of the penalty area. Putting the last of his strength behind the pass, he launched the ball into the box.

The crowd, which had been going crazy mere moments before, held their collective breath as the ball flew through the air. Gary hoisted his grandson out of the wheelchair and climbed over the ropes to get closer to the field.

The ball came down as though in slow motion. Davie never took his eyes off it as it dropped, which was probably why he didn't see the divot he tripped over. He flew through the air, his arms pinned to his side, and just before he hit the ground, the ball connected with the crown of his head and flew into the net.

There was a moment of stunned silence as everyone tried to register what had just happened, but then they erupted. They piled onto the field as the referee blew the final whistle, most of them headed for Davie, who was still face down on the grass trying to catch his breath.

Greig ran over to his son and swung him through the air. "We did it," he yelled. "Woohooooo."

"You were brilliant, Dad."

"Ladies and gentlemen," Colin called over the amplifier, his voice failing to cut through the sounds of celebration. "LISTEN UP, YOU SHOWER OF DIRTY BASTARDS."

That got their attention.

"Ladies and gentleman, could I please direct your attention to the VIP area for the presentation of the Graham Ramsay trophy."

The villagers applauded as the Scotland players made their way to the table, pushing Greig to the front of the line. He wiped away tears as

Graham handed over the trophy, grinning like the Chesire Cat. The rest of the team gathered around and placed their hands on the silverware as Greig hoisted it aloft to rapturous applause.

They passed the trophy around, taking turns kissing it and holding it in the air. As Malcolm finished his turn, he looked over the parking lot and said, "Who's that?"

A man in a suit and matching tie was stepping out of a stretch limousine. He stopped to talk to the driver and then walked in the direction of the soccer field.

"Does anyone know who that is?"

The man waved as he got closer, then walked over to Davie and shook his hand. "How are you doing, Mr. Chalmers? Hector sends his regards."

"What's happening?" Malcolm asked.

"I'm sorry I missed the game, but it looks like we got the win. Congratulations. My name is Stephen Miller, and I am here on behalf of Hector

McMillan and the Scottish Football Association. Could someone please point me in the direction of Graham Ramsay?"

The crowd parted as Lorna pushed her grandson to the front of the pack. "I'm Graham," he said meekly.

"It's a pleasure to meet you, Graham. We received a call earlier this week from Davie, an old friend of Hector's, telling us that you were having a tough time finding a ticket for the game tomorrow. Would that be right?"

Graham nodded.

"Well, that's no good at all, but I think we can fix it. Hector would like to have you and your father, as well as four guests of your choosing, in his private suite at Hampden Park tomorrow. We have hotel rooms booked for you and your guests tonight and a ride in our limo to and from the game."

"I get to choose?' Graham asked.

"Whomever you like."

Greig kneeled beside his son. "Who are you thinking, wee man?"

The boy bit his bottom look as he surveyed the faces in the crowd. "Nana and Grankie for sure."

The tissue made another appearance as Lorna dabbed at her eyes. "You're such a sweet boy, but don't waste one of your picks on me. I'm not too fond of football. Who else would you like?"

"Davie and Malcolm." Graham looked at his dad for a moment and smiled. "And Geraldine."

Geraldine moved around the front of the wheelchair and dropped to eye level with Graham. She took his hand, her eyes damp, and said, "I would love to be there with you, but I can't go."

"Why not," Graham asked, his bottom lip trembling.

"I need to go on a trip, but you know who would love to go?' She leaned in and whispered a name in his ear and then told him she loved him before picking her way through the crowd and walking away.

"My last pick is Hagrid."

The crowd cheered, and the big man beamed. "Jessie, you are in charge of the pub tomorrow. Do me proud," he yelled to one of his employees.

"Fantastic," Stephen said. "If you gentlemen would like to go home and freshen up, I can meet you all down at the pub in an hour, and we can get on the road then."

Greig took a moment to thank Stephen and then went after Geraldine, who was walking quickly towards the village. Greig's legs burned, but he ran as fast as he could, calling out her name. She stopped and turned to face him, tears streaming down her face.

"Where are you going?" Greig asked, trying to catch his breath.

"I'm going back to Glasgow tomorrow. I'm selling my mum's house and giving things another go with my fiancé."

"Is that what you want?"

"No, but I have no other option."

"You do. I'm staying. I've already talked to my lawyer about handing over the business. I belong here, and I want to be with you. I love you, Geraldine."

She reached out and put her hand on his face. "And I love you. I always bloody have, but I want all of you. I know I can never have that."

"Of course you can."

She shook her head. "What you had with your wife was a beautiful thing, still is, but it's been thirteen years. I want all of you now."

Greig dropped his head and ran his finger through his hair. "I've tried to let her go, but I can't. She'll always be a part of me."

"I understand that. Honestly, I do. But can you see how that might not work for me? I never thought of myself as the jealous type, but it seems I am."

"I'm going to miss you," Greig said.

"Same. Now, I really have to go." Geraldine turned and headed for the path that led down into the village, breaking into a run as she disappeared out of sight.

Heading back to the park, Grieg put on a brave face for his son, but inside, he was coming apart at the seams.

Chapter Fourteen

The bedroom window rattled as the wind did its best to break through the glass. Greig pulled the blanket a little tighter around his body even though he wasn't particularly cold. The rest of the house was quiet, save for the creaks and groans of the old place as it settled for the night.

Lorna and Gary were asleep in the room next door. His mum had argued about being sent away for the night, but Greig knew that both his parents were exhausted after three straight days of tending to Graham around the clock.

The trip to Glasgow and getting to watch the big game in the comfort of the private suite had proven to be the last bout of excitement that Graham's tired body could handle. He had fallen asleep on the limo ride home and had been in and out of slumber since then, his body burning up with fever.

Greig wanted to close his eyes, but he was terrified he would miss his boy's last breath. He forced himself upright in the chair, his knees banging against the side of the bed. The impact caused the bed to shake, and Graham opened his eyes.

"Dad?" he croaked.

"I'm right here, wee man," Greig said, leaning forward so that his boy could see him better in the dimly lit room.

"What time is it?"

"It's late. Are you thirsty?"

Graham shook his head wearily, the effort of the movement seeming to drain him further. "I'm ready to go."

"Okay, kiddo," Greig said, moving onto the bed to lay beside him.

"Will you carry me to Corbies Peak?"

"It's cold out there. Wouldn't you be more comfortable here?"

"I need to go there. Please, Dad. You can put Davie's jacket on me. That'll keep me warm."

"Okay." Greig stood and lifted his son out of bed, wrapping him in the jacket and adding a woolen hat for good measure. He quietly opened the bedroom door and stole a glance up and down the hallway. Once he was sure that the coast was clear, he headed downstairs and out the front door.

He pulled Graham in close as the wind tore at them. Following an old shortcut to the path that led up to Corbies Peak, Greig quickened his pace, trying to get some blood running through his veins to keep the cold out.

By the time they reached the bench overlooking the ocean, a thin layer of sweat had covered his body. He sat down, cradling the boy to his chest, the wind whipping off the water stinging his eyes.

It was dark, but he could make out strips of white on the ocean as the waves broke towards the shore, the water hammering forcefully at the face of the cliff. The sound of it all roared in his ears, but he still managed to hear Graham speak as the boy turned to face the water.

"Thank you, Dad. Thank you for bringing me to your home."

"My home is wherever you are, wee man."

"Dad?"

"What is it?"

"Do you see her?"

"See who?"

Graham reached out as though he was about to point, but instead, he pressed his fingers to his lips and blew a kiss out in the direction of the ocean.

"Is it Mum?"

"Yes. She's come to take me, and she wants you to be happy."

"I can't…"

"She's asking you to sing our song. Can you do that for us, Dad?"

Greig reached down and stroked his son's hair, following the boy's gaze to some point off in the distance. He began to sing. "You're the best thing that ever happened to me or my world. You're the best thing that ever happened, so don't go away."

He could feel the rise and fall of his son's chest against his hand, each breath slowly getting further and further apart until they finally stopped. Pulling his son in close, Greig began to sob, the howling wind seeming to share in his pain.

Greig stood and walked to the edge of the cliff, looking down at the raging water below.

He turned and looked towards the village he had loved as a boy and had come to love again. There was no way he could ever leave now, so he turned and blew a kiss across the rooftops.

"My home is wherever you are. You and your mum," he said once more as he and Graham stepped off the cliff and into the darkness below.

Acknowledgments

This book is as close to an autobiography as I will ever get, so I need to thank my wife Penny for supporting me as I cried several times during this trip down memory lane. I want to thank Erin Lee and Crazy Ink for giving me free rein to write the stories that I want. I also need to thank all of you who take the time to read my stories, even those that aren't soaked in the blood you all crave. The horror is coming back soon, so hang in there.

Born under a gloomy, grey, Scottish sky, it is perhaps no real surprise that darkness has always felt comfortable to John Watson. After countless hours spent in his local library, he found that he was more at home in the worlds of Clive Barker, Stephen King, and James Herbert than he was in his own. The need to carve out his own niche in the horror genre drove Watson to slice open his mind and let the words spill onto the page.

From donuts to mysterious karaoke bars in the middle of nowhere, Watson mines the depths of the ordinary to find the evil that lurks beneath the surface. He dares you to join him in his ongoing forays into the dark side.

John Watson's Novels and Novellas

Karaoke Night

Crueller

Off the Grid

Be Kind, Rewind

Cradle Robber

Slave to Blood

Anthologies

Infamy

Beyond the Jungle

Murder Maker

Made in the USA
Monee, IL
02 September 2023

42043765R00095